The Tweedie Passion

The Tweedie Passion

Lowland Romance Book 2

Helen Susan Swift

Copyright (C) 2016 Helen Susan Swift
Layout design and Copyright (C) 2020 by Next Chapter
Published 2020 by Liaison – A Next Chapter Imprint
Cover art by Cover Mint
Edited by Graham, A Fading Street Publishing Services (www.fadingstreet.com)
This book is a work of fiction. Names, characters, places, and incidents are the product of the author's imagination or are used fictitiously. Any resemblance to actual events, locales, or persons, living or dead, is purely coincidental.
All rights reserved. No part of this book may be reproduced or transmitted in any form or by any means, electronic or mechanical, including photocopying, recording, or by any information storage and retrieval system, without the author's permission.

THIS BOOK IS DEDICATED TO THE ONLY ONE I LOVE

Prelude

LETHAN VALLEY, SCOTTISH BORDERS
MIDSUMMER 1585

I traced the vaulted roof above me as I lay in bed, allowing the starlight to ease through the arrow-slit window and reveal the weft and pattern of the whinstone slabs. Stone is a good thing; it is solid, enduring. Stone never lets you down or betrays you like people do or promises one thing and delivers another like our Border weather does. You can rely on stone.

As the light increased, I could see the joins where the masons had cunningly fitted the great blocks together and I could even see the marks of the chisels where the masons had carved, following the grain of the rock to create tens of thousands of individual masterpieces that were connected together to form this Cardona Tower.

It was not time yet. I knew that. The stars told me the time by night, as the sun told me the time by day. It was not hard: it was just another skill that everybody had, like the awareness of danger or knowledge of the presence of a deer or a wolf. You learned these things in the Borderland, or you died. There was nothing else to it; all the lessons had to be learned and remembered. If you forgot, then your life was forfeit. Death was cheap in the old Border between Scotland and England, and life precarious. A man needed a woman and a woman needed a good man if she hoped to survive and a strong man if she strove to thrive. I was a Tweedie from the Lethan Valley; our aspirations rose above mere survival. Always.

I lay still, enjoying watching the light from the stars seeping into the chamber. I heard an owl hoot, soft through the night and the answering call of its mate. Male and female calling to each other, living creatures united in partnership although temporarily divided by distance.

That was the way of the world. Everybody needed a mate; every man needed a woman and every woman needed a man. I did not have mine yet although I thought I knew who he would be. I lay there, smiling, as I thought of him. My smile altered to a feeling of exasperation as I considered his faults. There was a lot of work to do before he was ready. I could mould him though. I must mould him if I wanted to survive along this savage frontier.

It was nearly time. I left my bedchamber and slipped off my nightclothes, so I stood naked by the window, allowing the air to caress the curves of my body. Lifting the wooden sneck that held my door shut, I slipped outside, glancing to right and left in case there were prying eyes. There were none; I had not expected any in my own home. The spiral turnpike stair was empty. I stepped out; enjoying the thrill of possible discovery more than I perhaps should even as my feet recoiled from the chill of the stone steps.

I reached the roof, where stone slabs protected the tower house from fire and the parapet offered sentries protection from any attacker. The night air was refreshing, with stars stretching into the unknown abyss of heaven. It was not full dark. It is never full dark in midsummer in Scotland, with the daylight fading only to a friendly grey that shaded the brilliance of the stars and cloaked the hills in mystery. They surrounded us on three sides, these hills, vague in the dim, with the opening of the Lethan Valley on the fourth, stretching north with the silver streak of the Lethan Water in the centre.

It was Midsummer's Eve.

It was my birthday.

I was twenty years old.

I spread my arms and legs, allowing the air full movement around my body, luxuriating in the kiss and caress, the feel of freedom, the knowledge that I was me and this was my time. Raising my face to the night, I opened my eyes and mouth as wide as I could to allow the spirit of my night to come home. And I waited for him to return.

It only happened at midnight on my birthday, Midsummer's Eve. In Scotland, there is a belief that people born at that time are special, that we have gifts denied to others. Well, I am here to tell you that we are not. I am most remarkably like every other woman in the land. I have two legs, two arms, one head, and all the other bits and pieces, bumps and appendages that I should have, all in the proper place and all the correct shape and size. Well, maybe I am slightly too ample around the hips, but I won't talk about that. There is nothing extraordinary about me in the slightest, except perhaps that I am as stubborn as the most obstinate of cattle, I have the occasional vision, and I can talk quite a lot.

I did not talk as midnight approached. I waited for the vision to descend.

I was in a shallow valley, with the wind whispering through coarse grass. Nearby there was a peel tower, slowly smouldering and sending wispy, acrid smoke to a bruised sky. I was lonely and scared, although there were many men around me. One man approached me; tall, lean, and scarred, he had a face that could chill the fear from a nightmare and eyes sharp and hard enough to bore through a granite cliff.

I backed away, feeling the fear surge through me, knowing that there was nowhere to run. I heard cruel laughter from the men around, rising above the crackle of flames and the lowing of reived cattle.

'Come here.' His voice was like death; cracked, harsh, with an accent from the West.

I did not come. I backed further away until whipcord arms stopped me, holding me tight. I was held and then pushed forward toward the scarred man. I tried to face him, to talk my way out of trouble but the words would not come. My tongue failed me when it was most needed.

'Come here,' the scarred man repeated. He stood with his legs apart, his thumbs hooked into his sword belt, and those devil eyes searing into my soul.

'I will not come,' I said.

He stepped towards me, slowly and with each footstep sinking into the springy grass. A gust of wind sent smoke from the fire around him, so he appeared to be emerging from the pits of hell. He let go of his belt and extended his hands toward me. They were long-fingered, with nails like talons, reaching out to grab me. I tried to pull backwards, to ease further away.

I was held again, surrounded by harsh laughter.

My nightmare was about to get worse.

The single shout broke the spell and we all looked to the west, where a lone rider had appeared on the hill crest. Silhouetted against the rising sun, I could not make out details. I only saw a tall, slender man on a horse with a banner in his hand. He stood there for a second with his horse prancing, its fore hooves raised and kicking at the air, and then he plunged down toward me, yelling something, although in my vision I could not make out the words.

'Robert!' I said and knew that all would be well.

It was the same vision every midsummer on the anniversary of my birth. It never varied in detail or time. I stood there, stark naked and now chilled as the image faded and the stars shone down in all their majesty.

'How had Robert known I was in danger?' I asked. 'Why was he riding alone?'

The stars did not answer. I only knew that my vision would one day become reality. Being born on midnight of Midsummer's Day may well make me special but the gift of second sight was a curse I would be happy to pass along to somebody else. All the same, I knew that at some time in the future, Robert would save me from an unknown band of reivers.

'Get back into bed!' Mother's voice was nearly as harsh as that of the scarred man. She grabbed me by the shoulder, hustled me down the stairs, and nearly threw me back into bed. 'I knew you would be up this night.' She glared down at me. 'It's time you stopped such nonsense. After all, you are twenty years old now.'

I looked back at her. 'I saw Robert again, rescuing me.'

'You saw no such thing,' she said. I watched the anger fade from her eyes, to be replaced by genuine worry. 'You'll find your man, Jeannie,' she said softly. 'And it won't be Robert Ferguson.'

The door shut quietly as she left my chamber, leaving me with my thoughts and the image of that lone rider. I turned on to my back, placed my hands behind my head and smiled. I knew that Robert would be there for me when he was needed.

Chapter One

LETHAN VALLEY
AUTUMN 1585

The laverocks were busy that autumn, singing their sweet song as we attended to the harvest. I have always loved bird call, from the liquid notes of the blackbird that sweetens the summer to the evocative call of the geese as they wing their way northward in the spring and return in the autumn, and that year of 1585 was no exception. I stopped my work to listen to the laverocks, trying to spot one in the vastness above.

'The barley won't gather itself, Jeannie,' my father said, 'so get busy with that reaping hook.'

I bent to the work, taking the hook in great circles that sheared through the stalks of the barley without damaging the grain. It was hard work but necessary, for every stroke added to our winter store and increased our security for the coming harsh days of winter.

As I worked, I looked around, savouring the valley in which I had lived all my life. We farmed in the traditional manner here in the Lethan Valley, with long rigs of grain set between those holding hay for winter fodder and strips of land left fallow for the following year. The rigs stretched from the edge of the flood plain of the fast-flowing Lethan Water and rose to the green slopes of the hills that enclosed us on three sides. To the east was Ward Law, the hill on which father posted a watchman to look out for reivers, for the devil and all his associates were unchained as the nights lengthened and the darkness encouraged theft, pillage, and reiving. Chief of our devils were the Veitches who lived in Faladale, over the waste of hills on the west side of our valley.

I saw my father cast anxious eyes to the sky as a spatter of rain dampened us. 'We'll finish this before the coarse weather comes,' he said, 'and we'll pray for the sun.'

'It's not the weather that concerns me,' Mother was twenty paces lower down the slope, 'it's that smoke in the air.'

We all stopped at the words, sniffing at the air as if we were dogs. There was only the faintest of whiffs carried on the fresh breeze and mingled with the scent of grass and late wild flowers. Father nodded. 'The wind's carrying it from the north,' he said. 'Peebles way.'

'It may only be a house fire,' I said hopefully.

'It may be that,' Mother said.

We both knew that it was not. The weather was not cool enough to light a fire. Smoke meant fire and fire meant trouble. September was early for the Riding—or Reiving—Season to begin, but that smoke was troublesome.

'The Veitches are riding,' Mother said and glanced at the spears we had piled at the edges of the field-rigs.

Father cupped hands to his mouth. 'Willie! Willie Telfer!' He had the knack of catching the wind to help carry his words.

We looked toward Ward Law, where distance made Willie Telfer appear very small. He raised a hand in acknowledgement.

'Is all well?' Father bellowed.

'All's well!' The words came faintly to us.

'Is there any sign of the Veitches?' Father made the word sound like a curse.

The Veitches, as you will have guessed, were the enemy of our blood, our name, and our family. Nobody knew when the feud with the Veitches had started, although there were many rumours and tales. I only knew that as far back as time, the Tweedies and the

Veitches had been enemies and always would be. The very name of that family made Father's lips curl and his hand reach for his sword, and I was sure that the name Tweedie had the same result if uttered in the foul valley of Faladale of the Veitches.

'No sign of them!' Willie Telfer called out.

'As well,' Father said, 'for if they were to strike when half the men were at the summer shieling, we would be hard pressed to fight them off.'

'The Veitches are also at the summer shieling,' Mother reminded gently. 'They will not come during the harvesting.'

I was not sure if I was more relieved or disappointed. Part of me was afraid of these devils, the Veitches, every one of whom was trained since birth to murder Tweedie men and ravish Tweedie women, but another part of me thrilled to see my menfolk in action, to hear the clash of sword on sword and see the brave deeds and bold actions. I had been brought up on the Border Ballads, you see, and believed in the tales of chevaliers and hardy knights. I also knew the sordid reality of cattle theft and torched cottages, as did we all.

'My Robert would see them off,' I said, more loudly than I intended.

'Your Robert?' Mother injected scorn into those two words. 'He is not *your* Robert, Jeannie my lass, and never shall be.' She shook her head. 'He is the younger son of a minor house and hardly fit to talk to you. Push him out of your mind, Jeannie, and cast around for a more suitable man.'

Father opened his mouth to interrupt and closed it again without saying anything. Father rarely gave advice about matters of the heart, leaving it to his womenfolk, that is, Mother and I, to say our hearts and afterwards make our peace. 'Keep them at it, Bess,' Father said and moved away. I watched him mount Dryfe, his stallion, and spur northward down the valley.

'You heard your father,' Mother said. 'We want this cut and the hay stooked before night's upon us.'

I nodded, caught Robert's eye and we smiled at each other. Despite what mother said, Robert was my lad, as you will know by now. We had known each other since childhood, or rather we had never *not* known each other. We grew up together, fishing or guddling for trout in the Lethan or the River Tweed, netting the salmon as they returned to spawn, racing each other to the summer shielings, working in the rigs or with the cattle, riding around the valley and along the ridges of the Heights. We were like brother and sister in some ways, and everybody and his mother should have known we should be wed one day. That one day would be when I was full woman and he was full man.

However, there is a huge gap between knowing something should happen and the actual event itself. Robert Ferguson and I knew we were right for each other and I had long since told him our plans for the future, but neither my mother nor Robert's father agreed. My mother said she would not let me marry until Robert had proved himself man enough to take a wife, and Robert's father, Archie Ferguson, just did not like me. I did not know why he should feel like that. I am a personable girl, active in what I do, and I am from good stock. Indeed, my family is better than the Fergusons of Whitecleuch or any other Fergusons in the Borderland between Berwick and Solway Sands. If bloodlines were to be compared, I can stand proud against any in Scotland, and that means any in the world.

As you can see, I am still indignant that any mere Ferguson should question my right to his son if I choose him. However, as we had neither lands nor cattle, Robert and I had to wait until our respective families realised that Fate, the Lord, and all the deities that may or may not exist in river, loch, hill, earth, and sky had decreed we were meant for each other. Or until some other man took my fancy, which was something that I knew would not and could not happen. We were destined you see, for I had seen it in my visions.

And therein lies my tale.

When Father trotted off that fine September day to seek the cause of the smoke, Mother took charge of the harvesting, which meant we moved faster and worked twice as hard. In the Lethan Valley, nobody argued with Lady Tweedie. Or if they did, they certainly did not argue a second time.

Occasionally I caught Mother raising her head to check the tenants were working as hard as they should. Sometimes she gave a grim nod of satisfaction, more often a sharp bark of reprimand. Once I caught her looking at something with a smile on her face and I followed the direction of her glance to see what amused her so. I saw she was watching Clem's Adam as he bent forward to his task. Clem's Adam was a fine handsome man of about thirty, with a face that many women spoke about and a body that would have graced any of these sculptures in the ancient abbeys. Yet it was not his face that Mother was smiling at but quite another portion of him that he thrust skyward as he faced the opposite direction.

Was a man's behind so interesting? I shrugged; slightly embarrassed that Mother should act like she did at her age and especially as she was a respectable married woman. She was too old to be thinking about men, especially men other than her husband, my father. I glanced over to Robert who was working in a similar position. What I saw did not interest me, so I saw no reason to linger.

'Keep working!' Mother had obviously switched her attention away from the rump of Clem's Adam.

If Father had remained with the harvesting, the rain would have beaten us. As it was, we beat the rain, so the barley was taken into storage and the hay cut and stooked at exactly the same time as the heavens opened and the deluge descended.

'Get back inside.' Father returned the minute the rain began in earnest. 'All of you. There are reivers about.'

'They are early this year,' Mother said calmly. 'Is it the Veitches?' Living on the Border makes one stoical about the unexpected.

'Not this time,' Father said. 'Much worse than that.'

I felt Mother stiffen. 'Is it the Armstrongs?'

'I believe so,' Father said.

Although Mother nodded calmly, I could sense her tension. 'Wild Will Armstrong casts a wide net but I have never known him to hit the Lethan before.' She raised her voice only slightly. 'All the women! Get the animals within the barmekin wall.' She pushed me toward the horses. 'Go along, girl. We will hold the tower.'

I looked at her. 'How about the kye?' The cattle, you may know, are at the shielings, the high pasture in the summer. Father had left them nearly unattended in the shielings so we could get the barley and hay cut.

'The men will get the cattle in,' Mother said. 'Move, Jeannie!'

She had made her decision and, as I said, nobody argued with the Lady Tweedie.

Our tower, Cardrona Tower, sits near the head of the valley, at the confluence of the Manor Burn and the Lethan Water, so there is a natural defensive moat on three sides. The Tweedies have owned the upper Lethan Valley since 1307 when our ancestor Sim Tweedie joined King Robert I against the English invader; before that, we only held Cardrona Tower itself. It is not the largest tower house in the Borders, but it is secure against all but a major army and all our tenants and most of their livestock can fit into the barmekin, the walled area immediately outside the keep.

Mother looked over at the tower, tutted and shook her head. 'I would wish for a better home,' she said. 'We are the Tweedies of Lethan; we should have something grander than a mere tower like any Border laird.'

I said nothing to that. I had heard the words, or something very similar, a hundred times before. Mother always had grand ambitions for a palace to grace our position as the pre-eminent family in the area. Father was quite content to remain packed and cosy within our gaunt stone tower. It was secure, it was traditional, and it had been our home for so many centuries that Father could not consider anything else.

Robert cantered up to join Father, looking somewhat bemused as he often did. It was an expression that irritated me.

'Take care.' I touched his arm, surprised as always by the hardness of his muscles. There was no need to say more.

His broad face broke into a smile. 'I will,' he said.

I watched him fondle the ears of his horse and check the sword at his side. He tapped his horse, waved to me and to my good friend Katie Hunnam of the Kirkton and followed my father out of the great gate.

'He should not need you to wrap him in cotton wool,' Mother said. I expected nothing more from her. 'He should be man enough to care for himself.'

'He can care for himself.' I watched the line of men ride up the pass toward Brothershiel with the horses sure-footed on the wet grass and Robert near the front. The rain increased, hammering off the barmekin walls and pattering into the fast-surging Lethan Water, a harbinger of autumn.

I had mixed feelings as I saw Father take the men up the pass into the high hills. Up here in the Lethan we were away from the worst of the riding families of the Borders, but we always had a fear that the Veitches would come over these same hills that Father was entering, and we did suffer the occasional raid. Only a year before riders from Liddesdale had passed us by to take the Thieves Road by the Cauldstaneslap over the Pentland Hills and hit the lands around Edinburgh, so we had been on alert. That smoke from Peebles had been a warning.

'I hope they will be all right,' I said slowly.

'Your father knows what he is doing,' Mother assured me. She lifted her hand and dropped it before raising it again to pat me on the shoulder. I could see her struggle between a show of affection and acting the stern matriarch of the family. I never knew which side of her would triumph. Indeed, I never knew which side of her was true and which was an act. 'You get back to your work and allow the men to do what they do.'

I nodded. 'Yes, Mother. Wild Will Armstrong is a killer as well as a reiver,' I reminded, 'and Father has not drawn sword or held a lance in my lifetime.' I hesitated, 'and then there is Robert…'

'The least said about him the better,' Mother said. She pushed me toward the door. 'The Fergusons of Whitecleuch have aye been a weak house, Jeannie, and Robert is as bad as the rest. Worse, mayhap.'

I did not agree but neither did I argue. I had learned from bitter experience that it did not pay to disagree with Mother. She did not reserve her tongue or her hands solely for the tenants and neighbours.

'Lock and bar the outer door,' Mother ordered. I hastened to obey, watching these men who were too old to ride and fight to push the great double doors closed and drop the massive oaken bar into its slots. It would take a battering ram to burst through now, and even Wild Will did not carry such a thing in his armoury.

If any raider managed to get through the outer door, they would find the livestock and many of the tenants within the barmekin wall, and then there was the peel tower to contend with. Mother ushered me through the press, with animals, women, children, and old men huddled together, all fighting for space in which to shelter from the damp night and through into the tower itself.

You may be familiar with the Border towers, and if so please forgive me while I give you a brief description. They are straightforward things, four stories high of solid stone. The bottom, or ground floor, is used for animals or stores, with the upper levels for living accommodation. The watchmen sit behind a parapet on the roof, ready to fire harquebuses or arrows at any attacker. Towers are cramped, crowded and uncomfortable as well as cosy and secure. It would take a small army to capture a typical Border tower, and Cardrona Tower is no exception. Many of the Border lairds have added a substantial house beside the tower to add to the comfort of the residence. My mother, as I have already hinted, had been pressing Father for such a thing all my lifetime.

By statute of the crown in Edinburgh, each prominent family in the Borders must have a peel tower within a barmekin wall, partly as defence against English invasion and partly to keep the Border secure from the raiding families. The barmekin wall had to be at least seven feet tall and two feet thick; not strong enough to hold out against artillery, but sufficiently stout to hinder an attacker. As the Borders were dotted with scores of such peels, they would delay any invasion, or cause the invaders to split or deploy his forces, allowing the King to gather an army to defend the country.

So, there we were, all locked up safe inside the peel tower while the menfolk hurried up to the summer shielings to bring the cattle to safety. I hurried up to the roof to peer into the darkening evening to try and see what was happening. As luck would have it, Mother had decided on exactly the same thing and met me on the roof beside the unlit watch fire with its tarred covering to keep out the rain.

'Who are you watching for?' Mother asked.

'Both of them,' I replied.

Mother grunted and said nothing. I knew what she was thinking.

'Mother, I am twenty years old now. If I do not wed soon, I will be an old maid, fit only to sit in the ingleneuk and sew buttons.'

Her laugh surprised me. 'I cannot see any Tweedie woman as an old maid,' Mother said. 'The Tweedies have ayeways been a lusty bunch, casting their eyes on every man or woman they fancy.'

I did not smile. I did not say that if the Tweedies were so lusty, why was I twenty years old and still without a man? Other women of fewer years than me were walking along the Lethan Valley carrying one child and with another toddling at their feet. Of my contemporaries, only Kate Hunnam and I were not with our man, although I knew that Kate had known many in the Biblical sense. I had Robert and was determined to wed him, despite the doubts of my mother who had continued to talk during my period of contemplation. I cast my mind back to what my Mother had been saying.

'You remember how the Tweedies got their name, Jeannie, don't you?' I had not replied to that question, so Mother had continued.

'Your ancestor had gone on crusade to the Holy Land, leaving his wife to look after the castle and lands. That was normal practice, as you are aware.'

'Yes, Mother,' I said. It was always normal practice for women to look after the castle and lands when the men went to war. That was how it always had been and always will be.

'Well.' Mother gave the secretive little smile that meant she was about to impart something she thought was amusing or scandalous. 'Your ancestor put a chastity belt on his wife to ensure she remained faithful to him.'

I nodded. 'That was not very trusting of him,' I said. I tried to imagine my reaction if Robert attempted to fasten such a contraption on me. He would learn that a Tweedie woman nursed a hot temper, at the least.

Mother grunted. 'I wonder if that lord intended to remain chaste while he was in Outremer. Anyway, he was away for five years fighting the Saracens, and when he returned, he discovered his wife with two children, the youngest only six months old.'

I shook my head in mock horror, as Mother would expect of me. 'The hussy,' I said.

'Hussy indeed.' Mother approved of my reaction, apparently. 'As you may imagine, her husband was not pleased to find he had been cuckolded. He immediately dragged his wife upstairs, ripped off her clothes, and checked the chastity belt. It was intact and only her lord had the key. His wife could not have been with a man, yet she had given birth on two occasions.'

I shook my head. 'How could that be?'

Mother leaned forward. 'It was obvious. As the knight's wife said, the Spirit of the Tweed came out and forced himself on her, at least twice.' She leaned back in her chair. 'And that is how we got the name, Tweedie!'

'Was it the spirit of the River Tweed?' I asked. Living in such close proximity to nature, we tended to be less sceptical of such things as nature spirits, hobgoblins, and witches. And do remember that I was born at midnight on Midsummer Eve and had my own gifts.

Mother raised her eyebrows wide. 'Your ancestor said it was… would you doubt the word of a Lady of the Lethan in such circumstances?'

I thought hard before I replied, which was most unlike me. 'Yes, Mother, I would. I do not think that any river spirit was the father of her children.'

Mother leaned forward and spoke in a whisper. 'Well said, Jeannie. You may make a Tweedie wife yet. Your ancestor's lover was a blacksmith; he knew how to open a chastity belt and make another.' Her smile was full of mischief. 'Men think they know all there is to know but we have the final say in everything.' She patted me in my most personal place. 'Especially what we do with that!'

I felt the colour rush to my face. 'Mother!'

'Yes, Jeannie: I am your mother and know what desires you will have and should have. It is the Tweedie Passion, Jeannie, and it is within you, waiting to burst out. You will know it when it comes and, God help you, you will not be able to control it. Rather, the Tweedie Passion will control you. It is in your blood, as it is in the blood of every woman and man of your name. Your father now…' Her voice faded away and she avoided my eyes, which was very unusual for Mother.

'What about my father?' I asked. 'You only had the one child and that was me. If Father was as lusty as you say surely there would be more?' I knew I was venturing on very dangerous territory.

'There are things it is best you do not know,' Mother said. 'I do assure you, Jeannie, that if you have only a fraction of your father's hot blood you will never lack for suitors.'

I smiled although I quite resented the implications. Let it be recorded that at twenty years old I was still intact where it mattered. I had never as much as kissed a man, let alone allowed one to touch me anywhere important. I told my mother so, tartly and with force.

Surprisingly, she did not react by slapping me. Rather she listened with a look on her face that may have been amusement, or perhaps concern; I was not sure which. 'Not even Robert?'

'No!' I turned my back to show my anger, thereby facing into the rising wind and cold rain. I was too stubborn to move, however, and endured my self-imposed discomfort. 'Robert would never touch me without my permission!'

'I see.' I was sure that I detected some disapproval in Mother's tone although it might have been disappointment. 'And have you never tried to touch him… even without permission.'

'Mother!' I spoke without turning around. 'You know I would never do such a thing!'

Her laugh was genuine, which surprised me. 'Not yet, perhaps, Jeannie, but the time will come when you will feel like doing nothing else.'

I snorted. I knew better than that. I had been around the boys and men of the Lethan Valley and knew what they were like. I could not imagine myself ever wanting to touch any of them in certain places until such time as I was legally married and had to perform my duty. Oh, they were decent enough lads, hard-working, hard-riding, some quiet, others noisy. They treated me like my mother's daughter, and some made sheep's eyes at me. But there were none that captivated me in that particular way. Indeed, there were none that captivated me at all. Although Robert and I were fast friends and engaged, I never had any physical leanings toward him. I was sure that when the time came, I would be adequate in that way, for I had all the necessary equipment and I am sure I had the shape a man liked. A wife had to accept her husband's desires, although Robert had never pushed himself toward me either. Perhaps after we were married, we would change; perhaps marriage would awaken some so-far-hidden craving.

I realised that I had been telling such things to Mother and she had been listening, nodding at all the right places. 'You will know it when it comes,' she said. 'You have not met the right man yet,' she said.

'I have met Robert,' I insisted. I was facing her. When had I turned around? I could not remember having turned around; what sort of power did that woman have to make me open my heart to her and face her.

'I know you have,' Mother sounded infinitely sad. 'Perhaps if he was the older brother, he may be a bolder man.' She raised her head to the sky and lifted a finger to quieten me. 'Listen.'

I heard it at the same time; the drumbeat of horses' hooves, echoing off the surrounding hills as they came hard-riding up the valley.

'That is not your father,' Mother said softly. 'He will be coming over the hill pass with the cattle. Those are riding men.'

Chapter Two

LETHAN VALLEY
SEPTEMBER 1585

For a moment I could not react. I was twenty years old and although we had lived with the constant possibility of danger, I had never experienced it first-hand. I had been too young to remember the excitement of the days when Queen Mary had been in power and armies had marched and countermarched across the country, and as I have said, the Lethan is a bit too far north to be raided by the predatory riding families and any Veitch raid had merely reived a few cattle or burned the odd cot-house.

Yet here they were now, reivers were loose in our valley and all its men were deep in the hills. All that was left were the women, children, and old men.

'Get the spears.' Mother was surprisingly calm. Raising her voice, she shouted out: 'Riders coming up the valley! Spears and bows! Take your places!'

We all knew what to do. Father and Mother had drilled us in case of just such an emergency, so we grabbed what weapons the men had left us and ran to our stations. I know I should have felt frightened. Instead, I found it all rather exciting really. Life could be so dull stuck up there at the head of the valley counting cattle and tending crops. It was good to have something different happen.

'Shall I light the beacon?' I had always wanted to put flame to the great beacon fire that sat in its iron cage on the roof of the tower. The purpose was to send out a message to our neighbours that there were raiders, so they could prepare and send men to help.

'Wait,' Mother said. 'Wait until we are certain. The reivers, if they are reivers, must have passed Whitecleuch to reach us, yet the Fergusons have not fired a warning.'

I bit off my disappointment, peered down the valley and waited as the hoof beats came closer.

I heard the hail. 'Tweedie! Are you in?' The voice came from outside the walls, loud, powerful, and a stranger. 'Adam Tweedie of the Lethan!'

'I am Elizabeth Tweedie of the Lethan!' my mother replied, equally as loud. 'Name yourself and state what you want in our lands!'

'I am the Yorling!' the claim was simple and direct. 'I want your gear and insight.'

'Oh, sweet Mary Mother.' Although Scotland had been officially Protestant for decades, mother still clung to the Roman Catholicism with which she had been raised. I saw her cross herself. 'It is a ghost, risen from the dead.'

I stared into the dark, hoping to see this ghost yet glad of the high barmekin walls around us. 'Who is the Yorling?' I asked stupidly.

'You will get nothing here.' Mother ignored my question as she shouted into the dark outside.

That same voice sounded from beyond the dark. 'I will take what you do not give me! I am the Yorling.'

'The only thing you will get here is an arrow through your eye or a spear in your stomach!' I hoped that only I could detect the fear in Mother's voice.

'Who is the Yorling?' I asked urgently. 'I have never heard the name.'

'Pray to God you never hear it again,' Old Martin spoke through a silver-white beard. 'He is the worst of all of them except Wild Will

Armstrong, a wild man from the Debateable Land. I am surprised he still rides.'

'So am I.' Mother had controlled her nerves as she spoke in a low voice. 'He must be an old man now. 'Let's see him.'

'If you are the Yorling,' Mother raised her voice again, 'show yourself!'

'I will do that,' the Yorling replied the instant that Mother finished speaking.

The sudden flare of torches took me by surprise. One moment the valley was in darkness, the next there was a score of torches flaring around the barmekin walls and down the Lethan Water. The horsemen who carried them were constantly moving, so torchlight reflected from the water and then flickered across the top of the wall. Except for the Yorling, they rode in an ominous silence that made them even more frightening.

And then I saw him. He was directly in front of the gate, sitting proud on a pure black horse. He was bareheaded, with black hair cascading to his shoulders and overflowing onto the yellow padded jack he wore as protection against swords and arrows.

Behind and around him were his men; I saw twenty, young and lithe like himself. With the nine-foot-long Border lance and with swords and dags, the heavy pistol, at their saddles, they looked a handy bunch.

'You are not the Yorling,' Old Martin said loudly. 'You're nothing but a cub!'

'A cub from the lair of a wolf,' the Yorling said cheerfully. 'Open up now before we storm the tower.'

I heard my mother tut in exasperation. 'Be off with you,' she said and reached for the bow that leaned against the beacon.

'That must be the son of the Yorling,' Old Martin was always good at explaining the obvious for the sake of those of lesser intelligence than himself.

'He will be a dead son in a second.' Mother pulled back the bowstring with as much dexterity as any Ettrick archer. She marked her target and loosed with a single flowing movement and the arrow sped on its way. The dark prevented me from watching its progress. Now, I can ask this without any hope of an answer: why did I hope that the arrow missed its target? This Yorling was threatening Cardrona Tower, our home.

I did not have to hope for long, as the Yorling moved sideways in his saddle so the arrow hissed past to bury itself in the ground behind his horse.

'Ha!' His voice mocked us as he pulled his horse, so it pranced on its hind legs. 'If that is your answer then Cardrona is ours!'

I do not know what would have happened next for at that moment Father arrived. I heard his shouting before I saw him.

'A Tweedie! A Tweedie!' And then father led all the men of Lethan in a mad charge into the body of the reivers. I watched in rising excitement as Father rode straight into them, as he had so often told us he had done at Langside battle when he was a young man. I had never quite believed his tales until that moment as he led the attack with a lance under his arm and fire in his voice.

'That's my man!' Mother said and I had never heard such love in her voice or seen such brightness in her eyes. It was as if she relived her youth as father crashed into the reivers. Unfortunately, as soon as the fighting started, the reivers dropped their torches so I only had intermittent glimpses of what happened as men rode past those torches that had not been doused in the Lethan Water.

I watched eagerly, looking for Robert in the press of horsemen that followed Father. Not all the men were from the Lethan, I realised. I saw Archie Ferguson of Whitecleuch there as well, Robert's father, roaring his head off as if he was twenty and not forty-five with a paunch like a woman near her time. I saw Bailie Marshall of Peebles as well and guessed that father had gathered all the able men of the district to fight off this reiver band. And then I saw Robert.

He was in the middle of the Lethan men, pushing hard to get to the front. I watched him, hoping he could sense my eyes on him. He drew his sword elegantly, hauling the broad blade of the backsword from its scabbard with skill. As he should, for we had practised it often enough on the green slopes of the Hundlestone Heights above Peebles.

I saw him open his mouth in the old Lethan yell, saw him thrust in his spurs as he urged his horse on and I had never seen anything finer in all my days. That was my chosen man charging into battle to fight for our lands and the gear of Lethan.

The Yorling saw him coming and I thought he must have selected him as the most worthy opponent for he turned his great black horse to meet him. I felt my heart race as Robert charged forward, head down and sword outstretched to meet the leader of this outlaw band. The Yorling did not charge but merely trotted, flicked poor Robert's sword aside and smacked his horse on the rump with the flat of his blade so it blundered past, carrying Robert with it. He vanished into the darkness beyond the sputtering light of the torches.

I heard my mother sigh and glanced at her. She was shaking her head sorrowfully.

'Come on, Robert,' I breathed. 'Try again. Don't let that Yorling beat you so easily.' Yet even as I said that I could not help but thrill at the skill with which the Yorling turned his horse, dismounted one of our men by casually cutting away one of his stirrups and tipping him out of the saddle, and readying himself to meet Robert's next charge.

'Go on, Robert,' I spoke louder, knowing that Mother was also watching, judging my man by his prowess against this vibrant intruder. The rest of the battle mattered nought to me. My entire attention had coalesced to that single encounter between my Robert, broad of shoulder, slow of speech, and the lithe, elegant black-haired Yorling with the bright yellow jack and the long sword that he carried with such grace and used with such skill.

'Go on, Robert!' I shouted the words loudly enough for them to be heard above the noise of the battle so that both participants in my own little duel heard and both glanced up to the head of the tower.

I caught Robert's eye and gave him a wave of encouragement, just as the Yorling kicked in his spurs.

'Robert!' I yelled.

He waved and met the Yorling's attack with a wicked swing of his sword that, if it had connected, would have taken that man's head clean off his shoulders. Instead, the Yorling lifted his sword to parry. I heard the clatter of steel quite distinctly from where I stood and saw the Yorling swerve his horse to the side and slice through Robert's stirrups, as he had done to that anonymous Tweedie a few moments before. Robert swayed in the saddle and tried to maintain his balance, until the Yorling closed, put one foot underneath his and tipped him out.

'Robert!' I screamed.

As Robert sprawled face forward, the Yorling lifted his sword and delivered a resounding whack across his rump with the flat of his sword. I heard my mother grunt with either satisfaction or malice or a combination of both, and then the Yorling was raising his sword high in the air as his horse danced on its back hooves.

'For you, my fair Lady of Lethan,' he said, kissed the blade of his sword, and saluted us. Or rather, he saluted me for his gaze fixed on me before he gave the most charming of smiles and, shouting to his men, galloped away.

I watched him go, marvelling at his horsemanship as he darted between Father and Archie of Whitecleuch and headed straight up the hillside with his men following, whooping and yelling as if they were demons from the deepest pits of hell that the Reverend Romanes so loves to gabble on about. That man was so thrilling that I watched him long after he disappeared into the dark. I wondered who he was and why he was here and where he was going. I wondered other things as well, but they are for my own private thoughts and should not be allowed out to graze, lest you think more ill of me than you probably already do. I knew that my Mother thought ill of me that September day.

'Well.' Mother broke my thoughts with her usual stern rebuke. 'Are you not going to see if he is injured?' She was watching me, her head to one side and her eyes narrow, wise, and all-seeing.

'He is all right.' I stared into the night.

'He is lying there groaning on the ground.' Mother nodded to where Robert lay.

'Oh!' I recollected myself. 'Oh, Robert!' And I nearly ran down the stairs in my sudden anxiety to redeem myself. And to ensure that Robert was all right, of course.

Chapter Three

LETHAN VALLEY
SEPTEMBER 1585

'Robert!'

He lay on his face, groaning softly. I put my hands under him and helped haul him upright, with his face twisted in pain and one hand on his haunches. 'Are you badly hurt?'

'Not too bad,' he said, trying to be brave. 'That devil in the yellow jack unhorsed me and landed a foul stroke.'

'I was watching,' I said. 'Luck was not with you.'

I saw Mother embracing Father, both of them chatting noisily as if they were young people in love and not grey-haired oldsters who should have known better and behaved with more propriety.

'I think he cut me badly.' Robert was rubbing at himself.

'You will have the luck next time.' I wondered if I should offer to check his wounds, decided that I had better not look at that part of him and offered him my arm for support instead.

'He ran too fast for me to catch him,' Robert said. He limped at my side. I saw his father and my mother talking as the men of Lethan dismounted and discussed the late encounter with rough laughter and much exaggeration. To hear them talk you would think they had won a major battle rather than merely chase a bunch of young callants away from the door.

'Come on, Robert.' I knew that Mother and Archie of Whitecleuch were discussing Robert's recent participation in the action. I wished he had acquitted himself better although I knew he had at least tried. He had proved himself to be no coward, even though he had been bested in single combat. I took Robert to one of the chambers upstairs and eased him onto the bed. He lay there, face down and giving the occasional piteous groan. I thought his wound must be causing him considerable pain and wondered what was best to do. I was loath to leave him yet unsure if I could help by remaining.

'Well then!' Mother bustled in, all decision and authority. 'How is he?'

'Not well,' I said, part aggrieved that Mother should interfere and part relieved she was there for if anybody knew what to do, Mother would. 'Robert's wounded,' I said, looking at her hopefully.

'I saw.' Mother did not waste time. 'Lie still and let's have a look at you,' she said and, without hesitation, dragged Robert's breeches down past his knees.

'Mother!' I was not sure whether to be shocked, surprised or something else as I had a sudden look at Robert's haunches all delightfully bare for my inspection. I looked, expecting to see a huge open wound gushing out blood. Instead, there was a faint weal, slightly red and with the skin only broken in one place.

'Oh tcha!' Mother tutted. 'Oh, you poor wee soul.' She stepped back, shaking her head. 'I am surprised you are able to walk at all after enduring that.' She surprised me with an expansive wink. 'Do you think he will survive?'

'Is it that bad?' Robert spoke over his shoulder, trying to squint backwards to view the injured part of him.

'Oh, bad!' Mother shook her head again. Suddenly tutting again, she looked at me. 'I've seen worse in an infant! Now get up and get along with you.' She turned away in disgust. 'And you, Jeannie, can see now why Robert Ferguson is not right for you. A woman needs a man, not a greeting little boy.' For one horrible moment, I thought that mother was about to slap him as he lay there, but she resisted the obvious temptation and instead hustled me outside the door. 'I do wish you would find a man,' she said.

Tempted to sneak back and watch poor Robert hauling up his breeches, I knew that Mother would not approve and instead walked into what we fondly called the Great Hall, from where a jubilant noise was emanating.

In case you have never been in the great hall of a border tower, pray allow me to describe it for you. As I have already explained, Cardrona Tower was no larger than many others in the Borders, a solid, four-storey, whinstone-built lump of masonry that would withstand the wind and weather for many centuries unless the English or some reiving band took crowbars or cannon to it. With walls some five feet thick, the interior was necessarily cramped, making the great hall a little less than great although it did extend the full width and length of the building.

With a vaulted ceiling above, and straw covering the slabbed floor below, logs crackling in the fireplace, and tapestries on the walls, the room was packed with men and women, children, and dogs, all laughing at their victory over the raiders and lauding their own parts in the proceedings. A piper enlivened the proceedings with his Border pipes until Mother sent him on his way with a cuff to the back of his head.

'It is surprising that with all that gallantry,' Mother said caustically, 'nobody got hurt. You did not kill a single one of the attackers and only one of us was in any way injured.'

'Who was hurt?' Father sounded strangely surprised. Did he think that such a victory could be obtained without blood being spilt? I thought he knew better than that.

'Young Robert of Whitecleuch.' Mother explained his extensive injuries to the now hushed room, leaving them laughing hard. When Robert walked in, the merriment increased, with the children demanding to see his battle wounds and Archie Ferguson scowling in embarrassment for his son. I sat in a corner, red-faced, wishing that anything had happened except what had actually occurred. I hardly heard Archie's near-casual statement: 'we captured one of them.'

'You captured one? I did not know that.' Again, my father sounded surprised. 'Where is he now?'

'In the black hole of your keep,' Archie said.

'Bring him here,' Father ordered. 'I want to see him.'

The prisoner was little more than a boy. He was about sixteen, straight-backed with a shock of fair hair and an expression of utter disdain as a brace of servants dragged him into the centre of the floor. We watched him with a mixture of amusement and trepidation. Was this an example of the reivers that scared us so much?

'He doesn't look much, does he?' Old Martin said. 'A callant at most. What's your name, boy?'

'That's my business,' the boy said boldly.

'That is a brave answer when you are surrounded by men you were so recently inclined to rob,' Old Martin told him and repeated. 'What's your name, boy?'

The boy pressed his lips together and said nothing.

'He's harmless,' Father said. When he pointed, firelight caught the heavy ring he wore on his pinkie finger. 'Put him back in the black hole or kick him out into the night and let him find his own way back.'

'Hand me that poker,' Old Martin said. He pressed it deep into the fire. 'When it is hot enough, we will ask you again and this time you will tell us.'

I had known Old Martin all my life. I knew he had ridden with my father when they were younger; much younger, and I had never seen him cruel before. I stepped forward.

'No!' I said. 'You can't torture him. He is little more than a child!' I felt the boy's gaze on me as I tried to defend him.

'There would be no need if he told us his name and where he came from.' Old Martin seemed amused by my outburst. 'Then we will know if it was only a chance raid or if they intended to return.'

I could see logic in that. 'We need to know your name,' I told the boy. He stared at me through level brown eyes. 'If you don't tell us, that man there,' I pointed to Martin, 'will hurt you sore.'

'I know,' the boy sounded very calm. 'I still won't tell.'

'Western marches,' Old Martin said at once. 'His accent gives him away.' He withdrew the poker from the fire, inspected the end and thrust it back in. 'What are you, son? An Armstrong from Liddesdale? A Graham from the Debateable Lands? A Maxwell from Annandale?' He reeled off some of the most notorious riding families from the western marches of the Border, with the boy standing mute.

'It matters not who he is and where he is from.' Mother took the poker from the fire and clattered it down on the hearth. 'He is a thief and a reiver. We have the power of pit and gallows in our own land. Hang him.'

'Mother!' I knew of course that we had the power to do virtually as we liked to lawbreakers in the Lethan. The Crown had given the Tweedies that power centuries before but, to the best of my knowledge, we had never exercised it. Certainly, I had never seen anything like that in my time.

The boy started and looked at Father, who shook his head slowly. 'Let me think about this,' he said.

'There is nothing to think about.' Mother had made the decision, as she was wont to do. 'He is a thief. Thieves are hanged. So, we hang him.' She pushed the boy toward Old Martin. 'Put him back in the Black Hole Martin. We will get rid of him tomorrow.' She clapped her hands. 'The rest of you: get back to bed or to your homes or wherever you should be.' She took hold of my arm as I moved away. 'Not you, Jeannie. We have something to discuss.'

Chapter Four

**LETHAN VALLEY
SEPTEMBER 1585**

When Mother spoke them, those words always had an ominous sound. On this occasion, she virtually dragged me to her private chamber and sat me down with a hard thump on the footstool while she lowered herself onto the chair.

'Now listen to me, Jeannie. I had hoped you would be over this silly notion you have for Robert Ferguson.'

Here we go again, I thought. 'It is no silly notion, Mother,' I said while wishing he had made a better show of himself. On our Border, a man who cannot fight is of as much use as a man who cannot ride. 'We are for each other.'

'He is not a man.' Mother was surprisingly patient. 'Look, Jeannie. We have been through all this before, time and time again. I am a bit sick of it now.'

'So am I!' I fought to control my temper as my voice rose. 'So am I, Mother,' I said in a more moderate tone. 'We have both said our piece. I am twenty-one soon…'

'And still with no more sense than when you were twelve!' Mother butted in, as she had a habit of doing. She stood over me, dominant yet with worry shadowing her eyes. 'Jeannie; you will find that you need more than just a companion as you grow into a full woman.'

I could see that she was struggling to find the right words as she tried to balance her feelings for me as her only daughter with her reluctance to admit that I would have all the aspirations and desires of a woman. Save that crucial one that I seemed to lack. I chose not to help her. 'Robert and I will marry,' I said, 'and there is nothing that you can do about it.'

I saw her stiffen; I thought she was going to slap me. Instead, she lowered her voice. 'If that happens,' she said, 'and you will notice that I say *if*. If that happens then you will be the owners of the whole Lethan Valley. You will have merged two of the most significant families in Peebles-shire.' Her face altered. 'I will not mention the *Veitches*.'

I nodded. 'I am aware of that.' I could see that she was struggling to keep her temper. Not twenty minutes earlier this woman had ordered the execution of a boy scarcely into his teens. Now she was biting her tongue in her anxiety to ensure that I did not make the wrong choice in a man. I did not then appreciate the depth of her love. I only accepted it.

'You are the only Tweedie of Cardrona and the Lethan,' Mother said bluntly. 'The family, your family, has held this land for nearly three centuries. You have a responsibility to maintain the connection between the land and your blood.'

'My life is not about that,' I said, as I had so often before.

'You are a Tweedie,' Mother said. 'Your life is about that. It is your duty and your responsibility to keep the land safe and the bloodline intact.'

I sighed. Would this woman never accept things as they were? I thought it better to pacify her. 'I do understand what you mean, Mother,' I said as patiently as I could. 'And if I marry Robert, I will have both the land and the bloodline.'

'For how long?' Mother's voice was flat. 'Your chosen man can hardly hold a sword let alone use one. As soon as the Armstrongs, or the Elliots, or even the Bold Buccleuch of the Scotts find out that a weakling holds the Lethan, they will rob you from Lethanhead to Tweed and leave this valley nothing but a smoking desert.'

I looked at her, wordless. The words were harsh yet true. Robert was no fighting man. And then I remembered my vision and I knew that all would be well.

Mother saw my hesitation and pressed what she thought was her advantage. 'Think on that, Jeannie, before you make your decision, and think of what happened to Robert earlier today.' She stood up. 'You may sleep now.'

I felt as if I was two years old as I crawled out of my Mother's chamber and into the cubby hole that I had for myself one level beneath the roof. Despite the busy day, it was very hard to sleep with so many images chasing each other through my mind. As I listened to the rain hammering against the leather shutters I had placed within the arrow-slit, I thought of poor Robert falling before the sword of the Yorling. Then I thought of Robert's bottom, strangely vulnerable on the bed, shining white except for that red streak where the Yorling's sword had landed. I knew that sight should have stirred me, yet it had not. I also thought of the Yorling with his flowing black hair and that supple skill with sword and mount. It was with that image that I fell asleep: that image and the sensation that he and I were connected in some way.

I woke with that same feeling and a faint smile that I did not wish. Robert was my chosen man. By thinking of the Yorling I was betraying my own choice and my own decision. Yet I could not chase the pictures away. And, if I faced the truth, I secretly had no desire to. I retained that smile until that other memory returned: Mother was going to hang that young reiver this morning.

I had never seen a hanging before although, God forgive us, they were common enough along the Border line. You may know that both sides of the Border, the Scots and the English, were divided into three Marches, or divisions. Each side had an East March, Middle March, and West March and each March had its own Warden who was responsible for dispensing justice in the case of disputes, and for putting down reiving. On the Scottish side, the valley of Liddesdale had its own Warden, the Captain of Liddesdale, purely because it was the most turbulent place in Europe, with the most predatory riding families, such as the Armstrongs, Elliots, and Nixons plus all the broken men and outlaws who belonged to no family or clan. The Wardens had one sure cure for lawlessness: the rope.

Now it was our family's turn to act as Warden: Mother had elevated herself to jury, judge, and executioner and that stubborn, tight-mouthed young lad was to be the object of her revenge. I was not looking forward to watching the spectacle and left the tower with a horrible sinking feeling in my stomach and dryness in my mouth.

I was not alone in that. Many of the women and some of the men seemed to share my trepidation as we gathered outside the barmekin walls. At the side of the Lethan water, there was a small mound with a prominent tree we called the gallows oak where traditionally these things used to take place, and we collected in a circle around, waiting. I sought out Robert, of course.

'I am not looking forward to this,' I told him, reaching for his hand.

He edged slightly away. I had forgotten that men did not like to show public displays of affection. Robert certainly did not. 'It's only a hanging,' he said as if he had witnessed scores in his time. I knew for a fact that this would be his first. 'A *reiver*.' He said the word as if it was a curse against God.

'It's a young boy,' I said, 'somebody will be mourning him. He will have a mother, a father,' I glanced at Robert with a hopeful smile, 'perhaps a sweetheart.' He did not respond.

The boy was silent as two sturdy men, Willie Rennie, and James of the Ford, hustled him out. They had tied his hands in front of him and hobbled him so he could take only short steps. Despite his youth, he kept his head up and his mouth closed. He did not look afraid.

'Poor little boy.' I wanted to step forward and comfort him. Mary's Bessie Tweedie was in tears: she had two sons of about the same age. I saw her looking imploringly toward Mother, whose face was set like flint. Others were watching in fascination as James of the Ford cut through the boy's hobble and mounted him on a horse, facing ignominiously backwards. 'What are they doing?' I sought Robert's hand. He did not respond.

When the boy was mounted, James of the Ford led him to the gallows tree as Willie Rennie casually tossed a rope over the lowest branch, which stretched out at right angles from the trunk. There was a murmur from the crowd with some people pressing forward for a better look and others holding back. Now that the time had come, only a few averted their eyes. One mother grabbed hold of her son and lectured him sternly as he jumped up and down, laughing. A gaggle of dogs barked around us, tails wagging and jaws slavering.

'I can't watch,' I said.

Robert looked at me. 'It's only a reiver,' he said.

I have never liked him less than at that moment. 'It's a young boy!' I nearly shouted. 'Mother! You can't do this!'

People stared at me as I pushed through them, determined to reach my mother and put an end to this horror. 'You can't hang this boy,' I told her until she nodded to Willie Rennie, who grabbed hold of me.

'You stay out of this, my bonnie lass.' His voice was like the growl of a hunting dog.

James of the Ford tied a noose in the rope and slipped it around the boy's throat so casually that I wondered if he knew he was preparing to end a young life. I tried to move to help, only for Willie Rennie to hold me tighter.

'Robert!' I shouted, hoping that he would come to help.

The boy held my gaze. He remained impassive, staring over the crowd as if they were not there. He looked at my mother without expression as she lifted her hand and smacked it down on the rump of the horse. It jerked forward so the boy slid off the back and hung there, legs kicking and face screwed up as the noose tightened around his throat.

'No!' I screamed as loudly as I could. 'No!'

I did not see from where the riders came. In common with the rest of the crowd, I was concentrating on the drama unfolding before us, watching that poor boy kick and gyrate as he choked to death when the storm arrived. The first I knew about it was the shout, 'A Yorling!'

I whirled around to see who had shouted that dread slogan. It was the Yorling himself with his long black hair flying beneath his steel bonnet and his yellow jack prominent as he galloped toward the gallows tree. The crowd parted before him like the Red Sea before Moses, and the Yorling's men followed in a wedge formation that split the crowd in half. I watched with a mixture of delight and astonishment as the Yorling flicked out his sword and sliced through the gallows rope. The boy fell heavily and rolled on the ground, gasping until one of the Yorling's followers jumped out of the saddle and cut the cord that bound the boy's wrists. Without any hesitation, as if he had expected no less, the boy vaulted onto the saddle of a spare horse and let out a hoarse yell of his own.

'Come to me, my dark lady of Cardrona!' the Yorling yelled and rode straight for me.

I had no time to react as the Yorling barged his horse against Willie Rennie, knocked him down to the ground, and grabbed hold of me with his left hand. Before I knew what was happening, I was face down over his horse and we were galloping past the gallows tree and down the valley.

It was all over in far less time than it took to tell. One moment I was watching the noose tighten around the neck of that poor boy and the next I was in a very undignified position over the back of a horse, a prisoner of the infamous Yorling.

Chapter Five

ETTRICK FOREST
SEPTEMBER 1585

Now, you may wonder what I thought and how I felt as I bounced down the valley with my face to the ground, my bottom sticking up and my legs kicking like an upended sheep on the heather hills. Well, to tell the truth, I had so many thoughts racing through my head that I would find it difficult to put them in any sort of order. Perhaps the first was surprise. I had never been in that situation before and it was not one that I had ever contemplated. The second was the sheer discomfort of it all. I mean, my whole weight was pressing against my tummy and the blood was rushing to my head. I was not a happy girl. The third was embarrassment. What sort of view did the Yorling have of me if he looked down? I had not chosen my clothes with any care that day so they were old and worn, hopefully not too threadbare in any too prominent place, and the Yorling would see a very prominent part of me right in front of his face.

There was no fear.

Why was there no fear?

I do not know. I have already mentioned that I felt a strange sort of attachment to this Yorling man. Now I was his prisoner as we galloped down my own Lethan Valley with his wild riders all around, whooping and yelling as they passed all the old familiar landmarks, which I was aware of but of course could not see in my head-down position.

I shouted out in protest, kicking my legs, and trying to punch at the Yorling as he guided his horse with consummate skill.

'Keep quiet, my lady!' He gave me a smack on the rump that made me gasp.

I called him a name that should have made him blush. Instead, he laughed.

'That is no language for the Lady of the Lethan to use,' his voice was deep, musical, and strangely familiar. I felt as if I had known this man for years, although I had only heard of him very recently. It was the strangest of feelings, but one which did not in the slightest prevent me from telling him exactly what I thought of him, his actions, his behaviour, his morals and even, may God forgive me, his parentage or lack thereof.

And to all of that he replied with laughter, or short comments such as 'is that so, my lady?' or 'I have heard that before, my lady foul mouth.' He did not attempt to slap me after that first time.

I could not upset that man in the slightest, which was unusual for me as even my mother had often told me that I was the most irritating girl in the world.

'Here will do,' the Yorling said.

We stopped and I was helped to the ground with more gentleness than I had expected. I stood there, stamping my feet, with my face flushed, sorting out my disarranged clothing and looking around at this outlaw band that had grabbed me in such an outrageous fashion.

I was very surprised how young they were. I doubted if any of them was over twenty-five years old and most would be younger. They formed a circle around me grinning or just staring as the Yorling himself slowly removed his helmet and shook his head, so the long hair rippled around his shoulders.

I took a deep breath. He was tall, taller than any of his men, and slender, with a long face and quite a prominent nose. His eyes were not as hard as most men I knew; they had a strange, near magnetic quality. Was he handsome? Yes, I suppose that he was, but it was something else that attracted me. I did not know what it was, and I certainly could not explain it, but there was that something about this man that immediately made me trust him. I have mentioned that before, I know.

'So, My Lady Lethan,' the Yorling gave a great sweeping bow, throwing out his right hand to the side and bending his knee. 'Here we are.'

'Indeed, we are.' I did not do him the honour of a curtsey. I said that I trusted him. I did not say that I was inclined to be pleasant to him. 'So, what happens now?'

He smiled, showing white teeth. 'Now, my foul-mouthed lady, I take you to my little home in the hills.'

'Oh?' I was very aware of all the eyes staring at me. Now, I quite enjoy being the centre of attraction, so I straightened the mess that my hair was in—hanging upside down over the neck of a horse does terrible things to your coiffure, you know—and faced him. 'And what happens when we get to this little home in the hills?'

'That is for me to know and you to find out,' my charming black-haired thief told me. His eyes were the brightest, smokiest green that I have ever seen. They held my attention as I tried my best to unsettle him.

'You are the one they call the Yorling, I presume?' I tossed my hair; I may have mentioned that I have black hair, and long. Tossing it always worked with the young lads in the Lethan. It did not work with this man.

'I am that one,' the Yorling agreed. He stood three feet in front of me with a broad smile on his lips and his hands on his hips.

I edged slightly further away. I hoped that I might be able to find a space between two of his callants and run for the hills. I knew the Lethan Valley and its surroundings as well as anybody, man, woman, boy or girl and I was sure that once I got away from these reivers I could lose them in the tangle of hills that surrounded the

Valley. Perhaps sensing my intention, the reivers tightened the circle around me.

'Why that name?' I asked, still trying to unsettle him. 'A yorling is a bird, a yellow-headed finch that is no good to anybody. Are you a small bird?' I flapped my arms and made what I hoped were chirping noises.

The Yorling glanced down at the yellow jack. 'I am named after my jack,' he said, 'and after my father, who was also called the Yorling.'

'A whole family of birds,' I mocked. I took a casual step backwards. 'Before your feathered father kicked you out of the nest, did he give you another name as well as Yorling?'

'Not one that I will tell you,' my enigmatic captor said. 'We have ten minutes here and then we are off. Is there anything you wish to do?' He asked the question with such innocence that I was not sure what he meant.

'No,' I said, 'except return home.'

'As you wish,' the Yorling said. 'You may wish to avert your eyes while I and my men use this time.'

'Oh!' I belatedly understood as he fiddled with the drawstring of his trousers. 'Oh, you dirty devil!'

I turned away to avoid the sight, only to see all the young men performing a similar act, luckily all facing away from me. I must have blushed crimson. I certainly felt extremely foolish to be surrounded by a circle of men all answering a call of nature. Naturally, I became equally affected.

'I will have to join you,' I said at last.

'Feel free,' the Yorling did not hide his smile. 'Don't let me stop you.'

Now my face felt as hot as any winter fire. 'I need privacy,' I said.

His smile grew broader. 'I will take you somewhere private,' he said, 'as soon as you ask me politely.'

I am sure that I stamped my foot with annoyance. 'You are nothing but a yellow devil!'

'I know,' he said, chuckling. 'Now: will you ask nicely? Or will my lads and I all stand and watch?'

I heard the ripple of laughter from his followers and knew there was no help for it. Swallowing my pride, I said, 'please may I have a few moment's privacy, Mr Yorling?'

'Why?' He assumed a face of utter innocence.

'You know very well why.' I did not like playing his little game.

'I will come with you,' he decided.

'You had better not!' I was becoming flustered now as my need became desperate and the circle of young men were smiling, nudging each other, and making suggestions that were a little too rude for me to hear.

'Don't be too hard on her.' I was surprised to hear one of the Yorling's followers coming to my help and looked around to see the young boy who should by rights have been hanged.

'And who are you to object?' the Yorling asked.

'She tried to save my life,' the youngster said. 'You must not treat her so.'

'Oh?' The Yorling seemed amused. 'I think I have the right with my own captive.'

'I have an idea,' the boy said. Before I could move, he had taken the reins from a spare horse and had looped them around my arm in a slip knot. He pulled them tight and handed the loose end to the Yorling. 'Now she can shelter behind a tree and you will still hold her safe.'

I did not thank him for his kindness. Instead, I slunk through the laughing circle of men and found a convenient sheltered spot. I tugged at the reins around my arm to find that the Yorling held them tight. 'If you look…' I began and stopped. He already had his back turned.

We rode on a few moments later. They sat me on a spare horse with my feet securely tied beneath and a rider on each side. Although I could not escape, my tongue was free, and I made the most of it. I lambasted the Yorling and all his companions for as long as my breath held out.

'I don't know what you want,' I said, more than a few times. 'I do know that you won't get it. My father will lead all the men in the Lethan after you. He will be organising a hot trod right at this minute if he is not already on his way.' A hot trod, in case you are unaware, is an immediate pursuit of reivers. A cold trod is a more measured chase that takes place a day or more later. 'My father will hunt you down and hang you like a dog.'

'Is that what will happen?' The Yorling sounded amused.

'That is exactly what will happen,' I told him. 'And my man Robert will be with him.'

'Oh?' the Yorling spoke over his shoulder, still smiling, still amused. 'Who is your man Robert?'

'He is big,' I said, 'Robert Ferguson of Whitecleuch...'

The Yorling's laugh stopped me. 'I unhorsed him already,' he said. 'He is no man for you, My Lady of Lethan.' He turned away, kicked in his heels, and increased the pace. I had no option except to come along. We forded the River Tweed in a spectacular shower of water and headed west and south into the Ettrick Forest, a tangle of bare-headed hills where patches of mist haunted the slopes and small woods of scrubby Scots Pine trees braved the never-ending winds, where deer floated away before us and burns seared the hill-flanks and formed barriers to free passage. I did not know this country and soon stilled my tongue as I tried to follow the route so I could come back if I managed to escape.

I was nervous as we halted for the night, and can you blame me? One woman alone with a round score of strange, lusty young men? Although I felt that strange trust with the Yorling that allowed me the freedom to lash him with my tongue, I had no such feelings for the rest of his band. I watched with some trepidation as the Yorling selected a place for us to camp.

'This will do,' he said.

We were in a corrie, a small hollow carved out of the side of a hill, with a circle of rocks in front and a small burn chortling at the side. It seemed a bit exposed for an outlaw band. The Yorling was either careless or very confident.

'We'll sleep here,' the Yorling said, 'and we'll be off before first light tomorrow.'

'Off to your secret tower deep in Liddesdale, my birdy friend.' I fished to find his name and where he was from.

'I am no Liddesdale man,' the Yorling said.

'The Debateable Land then,' I said, talking of the chunk of land that both Scotland and England had claimed and in which the worst outlaws and broken men made their homes among the local Graham surname. When either of the countries sent a force to clean it up, the wild men simply crossed the frontier to the neighbouring nation.

'Oh, not there,' the Yorling said.

I looked at his men as they dismounted and set about watering the horses and making camp. 'Where shall I sleep?' I voiced the fear that had been uppermost in my mind for some time.

When he looked at me these smoky green eyes were gentle. 'You will not be molested,' he said. 'My men will not touch you, My Lady of Lethan.'

'Who are you?' I asked. I had never known a man be so reticent. The men of the Lethan, and particularly the boys, were never backward in coming forward with tales of their own exploits. Every one of them sought to impress me with their skill in horsemanship and swordsmanship, in their ability to track or fight. Now I was with the most dashing man I had ever met, and he told me nothing, not even his own name. I was utterly confused.

'I am the Yorling.' He gestured to his yellow jack.

'You are the most frustrating man that I have ever met,' I told him.

'And you are the most beautiful woman I have ever seen.' His smile had vanished, and his eyes were steady. 'And the most loyal.' He did not drop his gaze.

The Yorling hobbled the horses with a cord tied between their front legs so they could graze at will without straying too far from the camp, speared a few trout from the burn and roasted them for supper and ordered two men to stand first watch.

I looked around. We were in the midst of a welter of long bare hills, where patches of mist slithered around the neuks and corries, feathering around the streaks of straggled trees. It was bleak, cool, and lonely beyond description, while the oncoming night cast a cloak of darkness over what was in truth a scene of desolation.

'Loyal to whom or what?' I asked as the melancholy of the night entered me.

'You are too loyal to that man Robert,' the Yorling spoke seriously, without a trace of a smile.

'He is my man,' I said.

The Yorling shook his head. 'You can do better,' he said. 'You need somebody with fire, drive, and energy; a vital man to stir your imagination and lead you to new heights. Robert Ferguson is none of these things.'

'He is none of your business,' I said hotly.

I knew that the Yorling was right, God help me. I knew that Robert Ferguson was slow moving and clumsy, used to getting his own way and spoiled. I had seen his mother take care of him all his life. As her first born and her only child, she had protected him from harm and hardship and the result was, well Robert was the result. Yet for all that, I knew that we would be wed and when a woman born at Midnight on midsummer knows, then she knows. There is neither logic nor proof needed. 'He is a good man,' I said, stubbornly.

'He is no man,' the Yorling said softly.

I had heard so many people say that, it no longer hurt. 'He is a good man,' I repeated.

'He is certainly not a fighting man,' the Yorling was smiling now. 'I bested him on two occasions without breaking sweat.'

I sighed. It had not been good to watch my Robert humiliated in front of the whole valley. 'He stood up to you,' I defended him, as I had done so often before.

'And he lost,' the Yorling said.

A sudden thought struck me. 'You could have killed him,' I said. 'Why did you not kill him?'

'It would have been too easy,' the Yorling said. 'It was more fun to wallop his doup.'

Remembering the contemptuous blow that the Yorling had struck I said nothing. He spoke only the truth.

'What do you intend doing with me?' I asked in a small voice.

'Holding you in my own tower,' the Yorling replied. 'You have had a long day and there is a hard ride tomorrow. Get some sleep, Lady of the Lethan. You will need it.'

He was right. I did need it although not for the reasons that he supposed. My dashing Yorling's plans were about to be thrown into total confusion in a manner that he had never dreamed.

Chapter Six

ETTRICK AND TARRAS
SEPTEMBER 1585

I heard the drumbeats of hooves and wakened from what had been an exhausted slumber. I sat up quickly, opened my mouth to shout a warning and closed it again very quickly. Thinking that it might be Father or even Robert, I lay still with my eyes open in hope.

That was perhaps the worst decision I had ever made in my life; or perhaps the best.

The horsemen came onto the sleeping camp like a torrent. They did not say a word until they were amongst us and then they gave a series of co-ordinated yells that raised the small hairs on the back of my head.

'An Armstrong! An Armstrong!'

There was instant consternation in the camp as the youths rose to meet this threat. I saw the Yorling raise his sword, to be instantly knocked to the ground; I saw the young boy who was saved from the hangman's noose bowled right over and others brushed aside as if they were stalks of barley falling before the reaper's hook.

'An Armstrong! An Armstrong!'

The cry rose like the thunder of battle, deep-throated, menacing like no other. Of course, I knew all about the Armstrongs, the most dangerous riding family in all the Borderland. Based in Liddesdale, that cockpit for half the trouble in Scotland, at their height they could raise three thousand lances and their towers and strongholds nailed Liddesdale to the blood-soaked ground. They terrorised their neighbours and raided from a few miles outside the royal castle of Edinburgh to deep inside England. Of all the reivers, they were the most notorious and the most dangerous. And now they were upon us on that exposed hillside deep in the Ettrick Forest.

'Horses!' a deep voice roared and some of the Armstrongs veered off to round up the Yorling's small herd. By that time, I had scrambled to my feet, staring. Things were happening so quickly that I could not make any sense of them. I saw the Armstrongs, tough, mature men, scattering the Yorling's young callants, slashing at them with swords and thrusting at them with lances.

The Yorling was lying still, bleeding from a wound in his head. Although it was he who had snatched me from the Lethan, I still felt that strange bond. I ran to his side, hoping to help. To do so I had to pass one of the Armstrong riders and he saw me right away.

'A woman!' he shouted, 'I have a woman!'

For the second time in two days, I was hoisted off my feet and plumped over the back of a horse.

'Stop!' I yelled, uselessly, and was rewarded with a hard crack on the back of my head that temporarily knocked all the fight out of me. I lay across the horse seeing nothing but stars as the Armstrong who had grabbed me kicked in his spurs and sped across that night-dark hill.

Only half conscious, I cannot say how long we travelled for. It may have been one hour, and it may have been twelve hours. I only know that I was aching in every muscle, hungry, parched with thirst, and totally exhausted when the Armstrongs finally stopped their mad canter across the bleak moors and hills.

'Get off.' The words were abrupt and followed by a rough shake that rattled my teeth inside my head.

'Who are you?' I asked.

'You'll know me,' the man said and tipped me roughly onto the ground. 'Or you know of me.'

I lay there, dazed and sick, wondering who he was until a hard foot dug into my ribs. 'Up!'

I tried to rise, but too slowly for my captor, who grabbed a handful of my hair and raised me to my feet. 'I said up!' He backhanded me hard across my face, drawing blood. 'Who are you?'

I looked around, desperate for hope. Instead, I experienced nothing but despair. We were outside a tower that could have been the image of Lethan, except for the armed men who lounged outside and the situation. While the hills of the Lethan Valley were cultivated and green, dotted with sheep and smeared with patches of purple heather, the hills I now saw in the background were dark with menace, scattered with grey granite rocks and reamed with the gulleys of intermittent burns. There was no beauty here, only grim rock and uncultivated moorland, with the tower in the midst of extensive moss. I knew without asking that this was the Tarras Moss, the last refuge of the Armstrongs and a place whose secret paths were known to none other.

There was a solitary dry patch immediately in front of the tower, with a piece of rising ground off to the right, where the Armstrongs were driving their stolen cattle.

The scarred man poked a hard finger into my ribs. 'I asked you a question.'

I felt inside my mouth with my tongue, searching for loose teeth. 'I am Jean Tweedie of the Lethan,' I told him, hoping that the name would put some manners into him. I may as well have asked to ride to the moon.

He grunted. 'You're a Tweedie then. Why were you with the Grahams?'

I did not wish to tell him that I did not know I had been with the Grahams. 'That is not your concern,' I replied and yelled as he backhanded me again. I fell on the ground, dazed. He picked me up again with his hand twisted in my hair and pulled me close. I stared into the most evil face I had ever seen in my life. The farm boys and middle-aged men of the Lethan were tough as nails and hardy as anybody yet compared to the viciousness in this man's face, they were soft-hearted innocents.

'Why were you with the Grahams?' He repeated the same question, drawing back his hand to hit me again. Now I know that I am stubborn, but I am not stupid enough to allow myself to be beaten to a pulp merely for the sake of it.

'I don't know.' I flinched, expecting another blow. 'They grabbed me as I was outside the tower and carried me away. They did not tell me why.'

The Armstrong nodded. 'Ransom,' he growled and looked closer. 'That's not their normal practice.'

I could not answer. I did not know their normal practice.

'It's a long way to come from the Debatable Land to grab a woman. You must be more important than you look.' He twisted my head back for a closer inspection. 'How many?'

'How many what?' I was aware of the other Armstrongs gathering round. Some looked curiously at me, others barely spared me a glance as they busied themselves with counting cattle and horses, the spoil of their raid.

'How many horses? How many cattle? What were the Grahams after when they took you?' He pulled me closer to him with each question, so I was pressed right against that wicked, flint-eyed face with the livid white scar that ran from the outside of his right eye to his chin and which writhed with every word he spoke.

'I don't know!' The panic in my voice must have been evident for the Armstrong merely grunted and threw me back to the ground.

'We'll find out.' He raised his head, 'Take this woman to the dungeon until we see if she's worth keeping.'

'No...' I knew enough about dungeons to not wish to visit one. Cardrona Tower had its Black Hole which was a small space underneath the storeroom. I soon discovered that it was a palace compared to the dungeon in which I was cast.

Ignoring all my protests, two of the Armstrongs grabbed hold of me by the arms and hauled me inside the gateway of the tower. I looked around, seeing a handful of slatternly women huddled around what I took to be a well and a stall of well-cared-for horses along the wall.

There was a trapdoor in the ground, which two of the women opened and I was tossed down, head first.

'You'll be in here until Wild Will decides what to do with you,' one of the women said, and the trapdoor slammed shut leaving me alone in the dark with my thoughts and my fears.

Wild Will. I repeated the name in my head; Wild Will Armstrong, the worst of the worst, and I was in his power.

I looked around me as my eyes gradually accustomed themselves to the dark. I had expected the dungeon to be something like the Black Hole in Cardrona, but it was fouler. There was a thin scattering of straw on the ground, enough to cushion my fall but not enough to give even a small measure of comfort. I heard the faint rustling and knew I was not alone.

'Who's there?' I tried to quell the faint quaver in my voice. 'Speak to me.'

Chapter Seven

TARRAS MOSS
SEPTEMBER 1585

'Good evening to you. Who are you?' The voice was deep and rich, with an accent I could not place.

'I am Jeannie Tweedie of Cardrona in the Lethan.' I did not keep the pride from my voice.

'Well met, Jeannie Tweedie. I am Hugh Veitch of Faladale, although I do have other names.' The rustling increased. 'Why are you held here?'

'Veitch!' I snapped out the name. 'You are a Veitch?' I pulled back in what space that horrendous dungeon afforded.

'And proud of it,' the answer came cheerfully back. 'As you should be of the Tweedies.'

I swallowed hard. Here I was a prisoner in a filthy dungeon, and my only cellmate was a Veitch. 'We are enemies,' I said.

'I have never met you in my life.' Hugh Veitch sounded remarkably cheerful for a man in a dungeon, and far too friendly to be a Veitch.

'The Tweedies and Veitches have been at feud for generations,' I reminded.

'So I believe,' Hugh Veitch said. 'I came from a different branch of the family, so I know little of affairs in Faladale.'

That was unexpected.

'I can see little profit in arguing about it,' Hugh Veitch said. 'We are both prisoners of the Armstrongs so it would be best if we put our differences aside for the present, don't you think?' He gave a little laugh. 'We can kill each other later if you wish.'

Remember that I had been brought up with tales of the cruelty and treachery of the Veitches. This reasoned and sensible response was not what I expected. 'Oh,' I said and relapsed into surprised silence.

'I will take that response as agreement,' Hugh Veitch said. 'How did you come to be in this unfortunate predicament?'

I wondered if I should reply to a Veitch and decided it would probably do no harm. 'I was a prisoner of the Yorling,' I said, 'and Wild Will captured me.'

There was silence for a few moments. 'I have never heard of this Yorling,' Hugh said. 'Why did he hold you?'

'I do not know,' I told him. 'He refused to say. Why does Wild Will hold you?'

'Oh, I am to be hanged.' Hugh sounded remarkably calm. 'We are at deadly feud apparently, the Veitches and the Armstrongs.'

'I am sorry,' I said.

'No need for sorrow. It is the way of things. It seems that the Veitches are at feud with many people.'

I could imagine his shrug.

'Well, I do not wish to be hanged,' I said, 'and neither should you be. Is there a way out of this place?'

His laugh was unexpected. 'If I find one, I will let you know, Jeannie.' I heard him move, 'but chained to a staple it is hard to move, let alone escape.'

'I am not chained,' I said. 'I suppose that Wild Will did not think it worthwhile chaining a mere woman.'

Hugh laughed again. 'I don't think any woman should be called 'mere',' he said. 'It was because of a woman that I am here.' I heard the rattle of chains and a subdued curse as he moved again. 'These things are damnably uncomfortable. It will be a relief to be rid of them, even to be hanged.' His laugh was short and not without humour.

'Can I help you?' I stood up, feeling my way along the roughness of the wall. I had only taken five steps before I stumbled over the top of him, standing on his right foot. 'Oh, I do apologise.'

'It is a small matter,' he said. 'I have another foot left.'

I felt around, grabbing hold of a foot, and working my way up to an ankle until I found the iron clasp. 'I can free you,' I said. 'It is a simple device.' I drew the pin that held both halves of the machine together. Hugh pulled his foot free.

'Thank you,' he said, as I found the second ankle and released that also. 'Now could you do my wrists as well?'

I fumbled in the dark, following the line of his hard, lean body. His arms were pinioned above his head, with both wrists fastened to staples that had been hammered into the stone walls of the dungeon. The pins were rusty and harder to release so I struggled, gasping with effort as I strained.

'I don't think I have the strength,' I said. 'I have a woman's fingers.'

'And a woman's compassion and determination.' Hugh encouraged me as I worked the pin from side to side within its slot.

'How long have you been chained here for?' I asked.

'I do not know,' Hugh said. 'I lost count of time. You're doing well. Please don't stop now.'

I felt movement with the pin. I pushed and pulled, straining against the stubborn iron until I pressed my knee against Hugh's shoulders for purchase and gave a final yank. The pin jerked out and I fell backwards to land with a crash on the stone floor of that dungeon. I lay still as the pain added to that caused when Wild Will had hit me. The filth and stench on that floor were abominable, as you may imagine.

'Jeannie? Are you all right?' There was concern in Hugh's voice. I heard the slight rasp as he dragged free the final pin holding his other wrist and then he was kneeling by my side. 'Are you hurt?'

'I am all right,' I said.

His hands were on my shoulders, strong and hard as he helped me to a sitting position. 'Thank you,' he said simply. I knew he must be suffering from the return of blood flowing to his arms and hands after being so long in a cramped position, but he made no complaint.

'Let me see.' Hugh's fingers probed my head. 'Nothing seems to be broken. Now we have to try and get out of here.' He stepped away and I heard him sit on the straw. 'You are correct; I have no desire to be hanged by Wild Will and I don't expect you wish to be his guest either.'

'I don't think much of the accommodation,' I said. I did not say that the company was entertaining. I was not that sort of girl. 'You said that you were here because of a woman?'

'That is also correct.' There was rueful humour in Hugh's voice. 'There was a woman who was desperate to ensnare me, and I was equally desperate not to be ensnared.'

'Ensnared?' I asked.

'In the trap of marriage,' my bold Hugh said. 'She was after my lands of course, rather than my not-so-handsome person.'

'Oh, of course,' I said, warming to this very modest man. 'And are you not so handsome? I cannot see in the dark.'

'And that is a very good thing,' he said. 'For if you could see me you would immediately know why Meg Turner would not be in the least attracted. I have a face like the wrong end of a bull.'

I laughed out loud. 'I have never heard a man say such things about himself,' I said, 'although I have heard many women make such statements—behind the man's back.'

'And quite correctly too, I imagine,' Hugh said.

I began to imagine his face, picturing the hindquarters of a bull and placing it on the shoulders of the man who sat opposite and in such close proximity to me. It was such a ludicrous picture that despite our precarious position, I had to stifle my laughter.

'Are you all right, My Lady Jeannie?'

'I was trying not to laugh,' I told him.

'Keep your laughter,' he said. 'You will need it when we get out of this place and you see what an ugly monster you have shared a dungeon with. It will be a story you can share with your children. All ten of them.'

'I have no children,' I said.

'Not yet,' he told me and relapsed into silence.

'You were telling me about Meg Turner,' I reminded, 'the woman who wished your hand in marriage despite your unfortunate face.'

'That's the one. I refused her kind offer of shackles much like these of Wild Will and she was very quiet for a space, and then she suggested that we meet once more to discuss things. I asked her what there was to discuss, and she said she may be able to persuade me.'

'And then?' I tried to hurry the story along, for Hugh seemed prone to linger at the most interesting places.

I could feel his smile even in that dismal place. 'I believed her. Call me stupid or call me simple but I rode along to the old chapel at Laverlaw, where the ghosts are said to flit and the moon pokes white from the blasted oaks…'

'Oh, very poetic,' I said. 'You should write that into a ballad.'

'I may do just that,' Hugh told me. 'I have always fancied myself as a balladeer!'

'You met the fair Meg at Laverlaw,' I reminded.

'She was not fair,' he said at once. 'She is dark; very dark; black of hair and black of heart. Remind me never again to walk out with a black-haired woman for they have natures to mirror their hair.'

'Oh,' I said. 'I will do that.' I did not tell him that my hair could not be darker. It was the colour of coal and so long that, when combed out, I could sit on it.

'I rode up to Laverlaw with my heart so innocent that I wondered if I was mistaken,' Hugh said. 'I thought of her wondrous smile and other things about her…'

'I do not need to ask what other things you were thinking about,' I said, once more stifling my laughter.

'No, indeed not. Women will also think about herds of cattle and fertile lands and the merging of properties together.' Hugh was a man of surprises. 'So, I was nearly prepared to be nice to her, especially when I saw her standing inside the chapel in a long white dress and with a circlet of flowers in her hair. She was like the Queen of the May.'

'How lovely,' I said. 'And she was equally innocent despite her black hair.'

'That's what I thought!' Hugh said cheerfully. So, I dismounted and ran forward, hopeful for… Well just hopeful.'

'I can imagine,' I said.

'Well imagine this,' Hugh said. 'I came forward prepared to be friendly and then two or three or a dozen other women of the Turner family came out of the dark, threw a blanket over my head, and trussed me tight as a goose at Christmas. I heard them laughing and, within the hour, I was handed over to the Armstrongs and here I am, my goose is cooked, and the noose awaits its next customer.'

'Unless we can get out of here,' I said.

'That would be the best thing,' Hugh said, 'for I have a score or three to pay off with the Turners.' There was little humour in his voice now, I noted.

'We are under the storehouse of the keep,' I said, 'and there seemed to be a great many Armstrongs in the tower.'

'Which tower are we in?' Hugh asked. 'I was covered by a blanket, remember. I saw nothing. Are we in Hollows? Mangerton, Whithaugh, Dryhope, Gilnockie?' He rattled off a list of the towers and strongholds of the Armstrongs.

Unseen in the dark, I shook my head. 'None of these,' I told him. 'We are in a huge area of bogland with the ugliest hills I have ever seen. I think it is Tarras Moss.'

'Tarras.' The name sounded flat even in Hugh's musical voice. 'There are only three exits to Tarras and the Armstrongs know all the byways and hidden routes through the bogs and forests. We are in the very heart of the Armstrong lands here.' He was quiet for only a few moments, 'and I still intend to get out. Will you be coming with me?'

About to say 'of course,' I pondered for a moment. I did not know anything about this man except that he was a Veitch with a sense of humour. I did not even know what he looked like, except that he was as ugly as the hind quarters of a bull. He was only a voice in the dark, a mysterious stranger called Hugh. Could I trust him? If I remained where I was, surely my father would arrange some sort of ransom that would get me free. No! I shook my head; that would not happen. I would escape here with this ugly man who had such a dislike for black-haired women.

'I will come,' I said. 'On one condition.'

'And what is that condition, pray?' he asked.

'That you do not hold my hair against me,' I said, 'for it is black, and there is a lot of it.'

'I will indeed hold your black hair against you,' he said, 'unless you forgive me my face like the wrong end of a bull.'

'I will forgive you that,' I said. 'We have a fine tupping bull in the Lethan herds.'

'Then we have a bargain,' ugly Hugh said. 'Now all we have to do is work out how to get away.'

'That may not be easy,' I told him.

It was at that moment that we heard the trapdoor above us creak as somebody dragged it open.

Chapter Eight

TARRAS MOSS
SEPTEMBER 1585

Have you ever had one of those moments when ideas just come to you? One minute you are sitting there with a slight smile on your face and your mind dull as a November sky, and the next you know exactly what you want to do. Well, that is what happened. I had no sooner told Hugh that it would be difficult to escape than an entire plan unfolded inside my head.

Grey light from above filtered through the trap, showing the feet and legs of a man as he carefully lowered himself down.

'Hugh,' I whispered urgently. 'Get ready to jump on him!' That was all I had time to say before two of the Armstrongs had negotiated the eight feet or so to the floor of the dungeon.

'Jeannie Tweedie!' the first Armstrong said. He was broad-shouldered and tough-looking, with a face marked with earlier smallpox. His companion was older, with a neat little beard.

'I am Jeannie Tweedie,' I said at once.

'Get up,' pockmarked ordered. 'Wild Will wants you.'

'I can't,' I said. 'I hurt myself when you pushed me down here. You will have to leave me.'

'Come on, you!' As pockmarked took a handful of my hair I looked up appealingly. Now I have already told you that I was virginal, but that does not mean that I am totally innocent in the ways of men. It would be impossible to grow up on the Border without seeing the various mating procedures of animals and people, so I had quickly loosened the top of my dress to expose my cleavage and more than a hint of my breasts for the gratification of the Armstrongs. I was well aware that I was playing with fire and the end result could have been disastrous and horribly unpleasant.

Pockmarked looked down and got an eyeful of untouched womanhood. I saw that his interest was instantly aroused as his attention switched from hauling me to my feet to staring at what I had on display. More out of instinct than calculation, I arched my back, tempting him further, and his friend came over to join him with his eyes as wide as they could open.

'Now, Hugh!' I said.

I need not have bothered. Before the words were uttered, Hugh had risen from his corner of the dungeon and, clever man, swung the chains that had so lately confined his ankles. With the doubled chain in his hands, he crashed the iron manacles onto the head of the bearded Armstrong, knocking him to the ground.

Pockmarked turned around more quickly than I had ever seen a man move, dragging out a knife from his belt at the same time. Unbalanced from his first blow, Hugh was at a disadvantage. I kicked upward, hoping to catch pockmark in an evil place. He hardly grunted as my boot instead made contact with his thigh, but that tiny distraction was all that Hugh needed. Dropping the manacles, he punched upward into pockmark's throat.

Pockmark opened his mouth to try and draw in a breath so Hugh punched him on the point of his jaw, knocking him to the wall, where Hugh punched him again. They were good punches that raised a thrill in me. I do like to see a man who knows what to do and does it well, with no wasted effort.

'Is he dead?' I watched pockmark slump against the wall.

'No.' Hugh took the man's knife and slipped it inside his own belt. 'Come on, Jeannie; time we were out of here before they realise what is happening.'

I nodded: I had never seen such fighting at close quarters before. I could only watch as Hugh jumped to the opening above us and scrambled out. Seconds later, he dropped a rope down.

'Take hold,' he ordered. 'I'll pull you up.'

I took hold as instructed but rather than wait to be pulled I climbed hand over hand to the opening. Hugh helped me over the lip, and I stood upright, looking around. I had feared that there might be more Armstrongs around, but the ground level was free of them, with only horses and various stores, dimly seen in the gloom.

'Can you ride bareback?' Hugh asked me.

'I've never tried,' I said.

'Can you? Yes or no?' I could sense his urgency.

'Yes,' I said quickly.

'Good; choose a horse; quickly!'

There were ten horses to choose from, all of the finest stock. Trust the Armstrongs to know the best horseflesh. I chose a fine brown mare while Hugh was making heavy weather of lifting the heavy wooden bar from the door.

'Let me help,' I said, taking some of the weight. He gave me the briefest of nods.

'On the count of three,' Hugh said, 'one, two, three!'

Between us, we lifted one end of the bar, and then it slipped and fell with an almighty crash on to the floor. The noise might have been heard in Edinburgh or Carlisle; certainly, it echoed throughout that isolated tower like the knell of doom on Judgement Day.

Hugh looked at me. 'That will waken the house,' he said. 'Come on, Jeannie lass, before the Armstrongs come!'

He hauled the double doors open and we peered outside. There were no guards, nothing except the cloak of night and the sweet perfume of the Tarras Moss.

'Why are there no guards?' I asked.

'The Armstrongs are secure here in the middle of Tarras. They are the only people who know the routes here, so they are in no fear of attack. Mount and ride, Jeannie; they are coming!'

I heard the noise from above, the harsh shouts of angry men and the clatter of footsteps on stone stairs. I saw Hugh grab a sword from a rack on the wall and then we were hurrying outside, with me insecure on my horse without a saddle, and the night welcoming us with its dark blanket and a cool smirr of rain.

Without knowing anything about the geography of the Tarras Moss, I could only blindly follow Hugh. Luckily, he seemed to know what he was doing as he led at a trot, looking back over his shoulder either to ensure that I was still there or to see if we were being followed or perhaps both. 'Can you keep up?'

'I'll try,' I said although in truth I found it very difficult to sit astride my mare with neither stirrups or saddle as we jolted through the night. To be honest it was a bit of a nightmare being jiggled up and down on that horse in the black without knowing where I was or where I was going. I wrapped the mane of my horse around my fingers, gritted my teeth, and endured the painful bouncing.

'They're following.' Hugh broke a long silence with urgent words. 'Can you walk your horse backwards?'

'Walk him backwards?' I repeated the words as if I were the class dunce. 'Why ever should I wish to?'

'Yes or no?' Hugh insisted.

'Yes, I can,' I said. It was a trick that Robert and I had perfected many years ago when we were very young people without a care in the world.

'Then follow my lead,' Hugh said. He reined up and walked backwards, keeping his hooves in line. I followed him, with my nerves screaming at me to kick my heels in and gallop away from the Armstrongs who could not be many hundreds of yards behind us. I could faintly hear their hoarse shouts as they encouraged each other forward and I could feel the vibration of their hooves pounding on the ground.

'This way,' Hugh said suddenly and broke off to the path to the side. I followed with my heart pounding and my nerves jangling as I expected my mount to founder into a patch of bogland with every step. That is the nature of the Tarras Moss you see; it has hidden stretches of deep peat-bog and sudden patches of forest so impenetrable that Jesus himself would struggle to find even the narrowest of straight paths.

'Keep in sight of me,' Hugh whispered, 'and keep silent.'

'It is you who is doing the talking,' I told him, more tartly than I intended as my mare slipped and banged me down rather sharply on his back. I gasped and rubbed at myself, wondering if I should have stayed put in the dungeon.

We moved on, with the horses picking their way slowly along the treacherous ground as the rain hissed down cold and penetrating. That rain may have saved us, uncomfortable though it was, for within a very few minutes it would obscure any trail we left.

I do not know for how long we rode. I only know that grey dawn was cracking the black of the night when Hugh next spoke. 'We will halt soon,' he said. 'There is a patch of woodland where we will spend the day.'

I eased myself on my uncomfortable perch and rubbed pointlessly at some of my aches. 'Would we not be better riding by day?' I asked, 'when we can see our way?'

'This is still Armstrong land,' Hugh explained patiently. 'We are on the bounds of Liddesdale. Do you know which families are there?'

'Of course I do,' I said, testy because of my myriad aches, particularly the major one on which I sat. 'As well as the Armstrongs there are Elliots, Croziers, Nixons, Turnbulls, Rutherfords, Laidlaws, Halls, and Robsons.'

'Aye, and they are all allied and related to each other; the most predatory riding families in Scotland.' I could sense Hugh looking at me although I was unable to make out his features in the dullness of that bleak dawn. 'Do you really think we would be able to ride through them unchallenged in the full light of day? One man and one maid, on horses without saddle or stirrups and with Wild Will looking for us?'

I knew he was right although I did not like to admit it. I was stubborn that way. I am still stubborn that way, as any who know me will bear witness to, but that is to jump my story and leave out far too much. 'No,' I said, shortly.

'Then we do as I say.' There was no triumph in his voice, for which I was grateful. Tired and aching as I was, I could not have stood any gloating from a man who had bested me in an argument. I would have burst into tears, or perhaps slapped his face for him. Probably the latter.

The patch of forest land was open at the edges and became denser the further in we pushed. The light of day was strengthening as we entered yet, within a very few moments, it was hard to see where we were going, so close-packed were the trees.

'Dismount,' Hugh ordered as if he was the Captain of a troop of the King's Horse and I was one of his soldiers. He watched as I very gingerly lifted my leg over the rump of the horse and slid to the ground. My legs wobbled when my feet touched the thick leaf mould, but it was that other much more prominent part of me that was causing me most grief at that time, and I was disinclined to rub there with a man watching.

I had no need to worry. Reaching behind him, Hugh furiously massaged his behind. 'I don't know about you,' he said with a grin that I could see even in the shade of the forest, 'but riding bareback really makes me sore.'

'Me too,' I found it easy to match his grin, 'I don't think I will sit comfortably for a week.'

There was something very reassuring about being with a man who was open about his weaknesses and I was much more relaxed about rubbing my own tender parts. 'I will wager that I have matching bruises on both sides,' I said more than I intended, and far more than my mother would ever have approved.

Hugh cut off his laugh. 'I will be the same,' he said. Mercifully, he did not ask if he could check, as some of the boys of the Lethan would have, nor look the other way in tongue-tied embarrassment as Robert would do.

'Now.' He cut lengths of grass, tied them together and created effective hobbles for the horses. 'We will let them graze and hope that if they are seen they look like wild beasts rather than Armstrong mounts.' He smiled. 'They were probably stolen from somewhere else in the first place.'

'I will call mine Kailzie,' I said, 'after a place I know well.'

'Kailzie she is, now and henceforth,' Hugh agreed solemnly.

I watched him work. The morning light was strengthening but in the gloom between these thick trees, I still had no clear idea about his looks. I wished to see this man who was so ugly that he thought women would only speak to him because they wanted his lands.

'First things first,' he said. 'I have to find a tree and no doubt you will too. I will head right, and I suggest you go left.' He moved away, stopping in the shade. 'Watch for the snakes.'

'Are there snakes here?' I asked.

'Not many,' Hugh replied quickly. 'The dragons killed them all.' His laugh was short and cheerful.

There was a small burn running through the forest, chuckling brown and friendly, with small pools and a number of miniature waterfalls. Hugh lay on his face beside one of the pools and slowly inserted his arms. A few moments later he flicked them out, holding a fat trout. He grinned over his shoulder to me.

'That's a good start, I think.'

'A very good start,' I agreed as he quickly put the fish out of its misery and slid his arms back into the water. 'Why don't you see if there are any brambles?'

I obeyed without question, which was highly unusual for me. There were a number of blackberry bushes on the outer fringes of the forest, with those on the southern side heavy with berries. I picked some docken leaves to carry them in, added a few very late and overripe raspberries for good measure and returned to the fishing pool to find the trout already gutted. Hugh was searching for dry wood.

'I'll start a cooking fire while you prepare the berries,' he said. 'It will only be a small fire in case the smoke alerts the Armstrongs.' He kept his back turned all the time, as if ashamed to show his face in the dappled light.

'Hugh,' I said at length. 'Face me.'

There was a long pause as he pretended to concentrate on his sticks.

'Hugh,' I said softly. 'You can't hide forever.' I felt the beating of my heart, as if I was in the company of some horned monster, or a Veitch, perhaps.

'As you wish, Jeannie,' he said eventually and stood up and turned around.

He was filthy and highly scented, as would anybody be after a long incarceration in a dungeon, and his face was bristled with a beard I judged to be three weeks in the making. Auburn hair curled past his ears to the level of his neck, unwashed and rank with sweat, speckled with straw and dirt from the dungeon. Yet for all that, there was nothing unattractive about him. Or there was nothing that I found unattractive. What other woman thought was completely irrelevant.

I held out my hand. 'Thank you for getting me out of that dungeon.'

He stepped closer, his eyes busy on my face. 'Thank you for getting me out of my chains.' He took my hand.

His grip was strong, yet gentle, with a hint of unleashed force.

'Who told you that you were ugly?' I asked.

'I have always known it,' he said.

I scanned his face. Nobody could ever call him classically handsome and he was certainly no Greek God. He had a broad forehead, filthy under his matted hair, and a pug nose above a mouth that the uncharitable could have said was a trifle too large. I preferred to think it was generous. High cheekbones only accentuated a pair of the steadiest grey eyes I had ever seen.

'Somebody must have told you,' I said quietly. 'In the Lethan Valley, all the boys boast of how handsome they are and how good they are at everything. Each one must be better than his neighbour at everything.'

'That is often the case,' Hugh said solemnly. 'If somebody were to catch a dragon, his neighbour would produce a box to put it in.'

'You do like your dragons, don't you?' I teased him.

'The constant companions of my youth,' he said.

I nodded. I did not have to ask why he had chosen dragons as his companions; all children need friends and I somehow knew that ugly Hugh's had been in limited supply.

'You were an outsider,' I guessed. 'If you were from Faladale I would know of you, so you...'

'I was not brought up in Faladale,' Hugh confirmed quickly. 'I was not wanted there. Or anywhere.' He looked away. 'I don't know why I said that.'

The pain in him was obvious. 'There will be many women who want you now,' I said truthfully, 'and not for your lands, either. I take it you gained them by inheritance?' I did not know why I asked such questions. Nor did I know why he answered them so openly. Most men of the Lethan lied out of habit; this man was very different.

'My father and uncle died of some fever. I was next in line. I did not even know I was entitled.' Hugh lowered himself to all fours and blew life into the fire. Wisps of smoke rose. 'If we are lucky, then there will be a mist to conceal the smoke.' When he looked up there was worry behind the humour in his eyes.

I knew I would not find out any more. It was time to change the subject and lighten the mood. 'I rather like dragons,' I told him.

There was relief in his smile. 'Have you seen many?'

'Oh, the Lethan is full of them,' I said. 'We can hardly move for the things.'

'I will have to visit sometime,' Hugh told me solemnly.

'A handsome man like you would always be welcome,' I said quietly.

'If he was like me, then he would not be handsome,' Hugh's smile was obviously forced.

I held those remarkably clear eyes. 'Whoever told you that you were ugly was lying,' I said softly.

Hugh said nothing. He took a flat stone from the burn and placed it on the fire with both trout on top. 'This will be ready shortly.'

I did not leave the subject. 'Send the liars to me,' I said, 'and I will tell them myself.'

His eyes met mine. 'I rather think you would, at that,' he said.

'If I was not spoken for,' I said softly, 'I would say more.' I could not add to that; I did not understand the feelings that were building up within me.

Hugh found another water-smoothed stone in the burn, placed a trout on top and handed it over. 'Not very elegant,' he said, 'fingers only.'

I tasted it. 'It is perfect,' I told him.

'It is burned,' Hugh said.

'It is not,' I denied. And it was not. A few moments later I licked the last of the fish from my fingers. Hugh was watching me through a fringe of auburn hair. When I met his gaze, he looked away.

'Best get some sleep,' he said. 'We have to get out of Tarras tonight and the Armstrongs will be looking for us.'

I had not realised how tired I was until I lay down beside a tree and woke up some hours later. I stretched, wondered why I ached in every muscle in my body and decided to stop stretching. Instead, I pushed myself to my feet and looked around. The light was beginning to fade into that deliciously sombre golden autumn glow, enhanced by the dead leaves that were falling from the trees. Everything was peaceful, with the scent of damp earth and faded flowers, a slight wind wafting through waving branches and the gentle gurgle of the burn.

I was hungry, so finished the last of the blackberries and found a sliver of meat on Hugh's trout. I also realised that I was extremely dirty. Well, there was a simple solution to that; wash in the burn. That raised one problem: where was Hugh?

He was nowhere near the camp, and the horses were unattended. They had not wandered far during the day and grazed happily at the side of the burn. I decided that he had either gone to seek more food or was scouting our route for the night. So much had happened the last few days that my head was in turmoil. I needed some time to think and somehow, I knew that we did not have much time. Eventually, the Armstrongs would tighten the noose, quite literally too. First things first, I had to get washed and get the muck out of my hair.

With Hugh absent, I needed to find a secluded spot on the burn. I would not go downstream into the open land of the moss where the Armstrongs could well be out on patrol or reiving business, so instead, I pushed deeper into the woodland.

I smiled at the sound of splashing ahead: a waterfall would be the perfect place to wash. The closer I moved the pricklier and dirty I felt until I was frantic to strip my clothes off and plunge into fresh, cool water. I passed a twisted silver birch, whose branches stretched right across the burn, and stopped. Somebody else had thought of bathing first: I had found Hugh and the sight made me widen my eyes.

I stepped back behind the cover of the birch, knowing that I should not watch but having no intention of walking away or letting Hugh know that I was there. Instead, I settled myself comfortably as a late-evening shaft of sunlight dappled a wondrous little glade where the thin white thread of the waterfall tinkled happily down and Hugh bathed, unaware of my presence.

In his unclad condition, he seemed taller than I had thought: a shade over six foot, and broader in the shoulder and chest than I had thought. I watched as he stood waist-deep beside the surge of the waterfall that thundered between two moss-furred rocks to descend twenty feet into a rock-lined pool, feathered with ferns and bright with that evening sun. He turned away from me with the water foaming around him, and the muscles of his back glistening wet. Raising his arms high, he stepped right under the fall. The water cascaded over him as he looked upward, scrubbing his hands through his hair and over his face, trying to remove the filth of the dungeon.

I had never seen a man take such care to be clean before. The boys I knew were perfunctory at best when they washed. It was quite fascinating to see Hugh in this situation, with his auburn hair sleeked to his head and his upper body a-shimmer beneath the foaming water: it was a sight I knew I would always remember. He stepped back from the waterfall and crouched with his hands busy underneath the water. I felt my mouth open as I realised which parts of him he was washing and stifled a giggle. I had not thought, but of course, men had to wash those places as well. Or some men anyway.

Without looking around, Hugh walked to the edge of the burn and onto the bank. He was all man and that is all that I will say about my first view of him totally unclothed. I felt my heartbeat increase as he strode to the clothes he had piled at the side of the water. He turned his back, giving me a glorious view of the rippling muscles of his back and slender, muscular buttocks that held my attention for an unconscionable length of time. All Borderers are bred to the saddle and that gives us fine legs and firm bottoms, yet this was the first time in my life that I was affected by the sight. I felt the pace of my heart increase as the breath caught in my throat.

At first, I was unsure what he was doing until I saw him take his clothes one by one to the water and scrub them between his hands before squeezing them dry. I was not sure why I found that interesting, but I did. Finally, when he had his washed clothes in a neat pile at his side, Hugh slid the knife from its sheath, splashed his face and began to shave. Have you ever watched a man shave? His face goes through a thousand contortions as he searches for every last elusive hair and patch of stubble. Hugh thought he was ugly; I only thought he looked comical as he shaved and I felt strangely proprietorial as I watched, almost as if I owned part of him, as if this strange, naked, not-handsome man was... was what? As if this man was mine?

I knew he was not. *Robert* was mine; I had known that since first I had my vision when I was around five years old. That was immutable, inviolable; whatever strange emotions I felt for Hugh, he could never be mine.

Nor could the Yorling be mine, despite the feeling of closeness and trust that I had immediately felt for that gallant young man. My emotions for that black-haired young gallant had been different again, although I could not find the words to describe them.

'You can come out now,' Hugh spoke loudly. 'Jeannie; you can come out from behind that birch tree.' He stood naked and unashamed beside the burn, looking in my direction.

Oh, dear God in heaven! He knew I was watching!

I came out, feeling very silly and very small.

'You will want to wash now,' this amazing man said. 'Be careful as you approach the waterfall; there are some slippery stones underfoot.'

I am sure my mouth gaped open as I stood there, saying nothing. Hugh lifted his still damp clothes, draped them over his arm and walked slowly toward our camp. Despite my embarrassment, I watched every movement of his body. He spoke over his shoulder. 'I will get us something to eat before we set off.'

I did not know what to say. If anything, I felt embarrassed, even ashamed at having watched him, yet I would not have missed those few moments for the world. Even now as I look back, after years of marriage, I remember how I felt watching Hugh Veitch at that waterfall.

I washed without enthusiasm, aware that Hugh was in the vicinity, part hoping that he would sneak up to watch me yet desperately hoping he did not. I knew, somehow, that he would not; he was a true gentleman, damn him. As I have written elsewhere, being born at midnight on Midsummer's Eve could be a blessing or a curse. Those feelings, those insights of knowledge, could be very uncomfortable.

We did not talk much as we prepared to leave that forest. I avoided Hugh's eyes through shame, and he was silent; I thought he was angry. Perhaps he was. He may also have been amused. I still am not sure.

'You look even better when you are washed and shiny,' Hugh said at length as he readied the horses.

'Thank you.' I touched my hair. 'Even with my long black hair?'

'It suits you,' he said.

'Does that mean it suits my black heart?' I fished for his true thoughts, or perhaps for a compliment.

'I mean it suits you,' he said. 'There were two parties of Armstrongs in the Moss during the day.'

'They did not see us.' I hoped to break the stiffness and return to something of the easy familiarity of the night before.

'They did not.' He closed that conversation and that hope.

As I climbed on to Kailzie all my aches and pains returned. I looked across to Hugh, about to make some jocular remark. His face was set, without humour. I wished that things were otherwise, yet I knew that it was better this way. The strange feelings that I had developing within me could not be realised. Hugh was a passing stranger; no more.

We rode into the arms of the night and I was very unhappy.

Chapter Nine

TARRAS MOSS
SEPTEMBER 1585

A betraying moon cast pale light over a scene of haunting desolation, with rough heather moorland between long patches of sucking bog and the occasional stunted tree. A hunting owl called, reminding me of my own Lethan Valley and I felt suddenly homesick for the sweet grass and friendliness of home.

Mother would be worried silly for me and Father would have called up the men of the Lethan to scour the Border for the Yorling. He would not know that I had been abducted by Wild Will and then escaped, to wander the wastes of Tarras with this man who was not ugly at all.

'Wait!' The man who was not ugly put a quiet hand on the nose of my horse.

I waited without question.

'Dismount.'

I dismounted, wincing at the pain that stretching some tender parts of me caused. Hugh pulled his horse to lie prone and I followed. Having a horse obey you was a thing all Borderers could do. There was no praise in horsemanship; you either managed your horse or you died. There was no other choice in the long hills and sweet green valleys of the Borderland.

We lay in silence, saying nothing. I smelled the acrid scent of a man's sweat, heard the low murmur of conversation and then the jingle of bit and bridle. Fifty yards away a man rode past, followed by another, and another. They rode soft and slowly with the nine-foot lances of the Border held ready in their right hands and the moon glinting from the steel helmets. I held my breath, closed one hand over the muzzle of Kailzie and watched.

The riders passed, one by one, each man looking about him, each face hawk-wary, hard, and set. Backswords swung low from their saddles, some carried a dag, the heavy pistol whose shot would tear a fist-sized hole in a man. And then they were gone, near silent in the night. I made to rise but Hugh's hand gestured for me to stay. His eyes were urgent.

I settled back down, aware of the insistent hammering of my heart and the sudden dryness of my mouth. We waited as a cloud skiffed across the moon, bringing temporary intense darkness. There was the soft scuff of hooves, the aroma of horse and a lone rider passed us, just as moonshine returned. I looked up. It was Wild Will himself, with that livid white scar down the side of his face and his eyes like gimlets, boring into the night.

My horse shifted, the sound seeming to carry for miles in the hush, and then Wild Will passed on with the hooves of his horse strangely muffled and his aura of evil shivering my bones. I took a deep breath, gasped for air, and felt Hugh's hand reassuringly on my arm.

'Are you all right?' His voice was soft.

I nodded, unable to speak.

'Give them a few more minutes,' Hugh said.

I nodded again. I doubt I would have been able to move at that moment. I looked sideways at Hugh. He was peering into the dark, concentrating hard. I waited, listening to the sough of the wind through the heather. That owl was silent now.

'Right.' Hugh touched my arm.

We rode on, slowly, looking around us, wary, alert for every sound, every movement. We both knew that the Armstrongs were hunting for us and Wild Will would hang Hugh without a qualm. I quailed to think what he would do to me. Always imaginative, my mind filled with images, each one more horrific than the last until I realised that I was scaring myself to numb futility.

'Wait…' Hugh's voice broke my thoughts. 'I've taken us the wrong road.'

I nodded. Not many men would have admitted their fault so openly. Robert would have tried to put the blame on me, or the dark, or the weather. I chased that thought away: I should not compare Robert with Hugh; they were two different people, each with good points and bad.

'Turn around; slowly now,' Hugh said.

I tried to obey, only to find that Kailzie's hooves were sinking in something softer than mud.

'We're in a bog,' I said.

'Wait.' Hugh slid from his horse and came toward me. 'Dismount.' I did so, fighting my fear as I felt the suck of peat-bog under my feet. 'Take three steps back, slowly.'

I did so and sighed as the ground was immediately firmer. I felt the spring of heather under me.

'Stay there,' Hugh spoke quietly so his words did not carry through the hush of the night. I watched his shadowy shape move back into the bog where Kailzie was neighing in fear as she felt the ground sucking her in. Blowing into the nostrils of my horse and fondling her ears, Hugh calmed her down before leading her one slow step at a time out of the bogland.

'Fondle her,' he ordered and returned for his own horse. 'That was an unpleasant few moments,' he said. 'We will try this way unless you can think of another?'

'No,' I said, smoothing my hand along Kailzie's muzzle, fondling her ears, and blowing into her nostrils until she nuzzled me. 'You know the area better than I do.'

We moved on again, ever more wary. Twice more we stopped as I thought I heard riders. The first was a lone deer, the second was a riderless horse, tossing its mane as it picked its own path through the Moss. We kept on, slowly, as the moon passed across the sky and faded, and a bright weather-gleam cracked open the eastern sky.

'Dawn,' Hugh said briefly. 'I had hoped to be out of Tarras before now.'

This time there was no friendly woodland in which to shelter from the dangers of daylight. Instead, Hugh led us to a slight ridge on which there was a peculiar rock formation. Two long fangs of rock faced each other, creating a cave-like effect except lacking a roof.

'This is the Wolf Craigs,' Hugh told me, 'because it is shaped like the jaws of a wolf.'

He was right; the edges of the rock were serrated like teeth, even the colour, becoming visible in the growing light, was ochre-red, like old blood. Sheep and wild beasts had used this place for shelter, creating a familiar, friendly aroma. Once again, we knee-haltered the horses, ate what little we had and settled ourselves in for the night. I did not mention the aches in my rump: not that morning.

'It is more exposed here,' Hugh said. 'We will have to stand watches in case somebody comes.'

I nodded. We relapsed into silence that I, for one, found miserable. 'Hugh,' I said at last, 'I should not have watched you at the waterfall.'

'No,' he said, 'you should not have.'

Well, that did not help much. I had hoped that he would say it was all right, or something equally placating. I felt worse rather than better; that man had a way of saying little and meaning much, rather than most men who talk a lot and say nothing.

'I am sorry.' I had to tear the words from inside me. I was not good at apologising.

He looked at me through these steady grey eyes and nodded.

I wondered what he was thinking. 'If you knew I was watching, why did you not tell me, or cover yourself up?'

'Why should I do that?' he said at once. 'It was up to you to look elsewhere, not up to me to hide away.'

'You did not mind me seeing?' I said.

'No.' His smile was slow but worth waiting for. 'I did not mind at all. You had seen the worst of me in my face; the rest is just like other men. If you wanted to look then you may look, and no harm done.'

I wondered if he was offering to strip for me. I hoped not. I would have expected such an offer from the boys of the Lethan, not from Hugh. 'I don't want to look just now,' I countered quickly. I was not telling the truth. I did not tell him that he was not like other men: no other man could have affected me as he had.

'I am glad to hear it.' Hugh quietened my fears. 'You are not the first woman to see me like that.'

'Oh?' I felt an unaccountable twist of jealousy for these unknown women who had seen him naked. I did not know why I felt that way. 'I don't wish to hear of your no-doubt many amorous conquests.' The bitter words were out before I could stop them.

'I have had no amorous conquests,' he told me with surprising frankness. 'Ugly men do not.'

'You are not ugly,' I said softly, and with force.

'Others disagree.'

'Then they are wrong,' I said.

'Other men are more handsome.' Hugh seemed determined to prove his own unsuitability.

I was equally determined to disprove it. 'I do not care about other men, and I cannot tell if they are handsome or not. Nor should you.' I took a deep breath. 'You have no reason to be shy about your appearance. Or your body.'

He held my gaze. 'I have three sisters,' he said at length. 'They are the women of whom I spoke.'

I do not know why I felt a surge of relief. 'You should have said!'

'You should not have looked.' Hugh was smiling again.

'I am not your sister to be teased.' I felt the heat in my voice as I stood up. This not-ugly man was playing with me.

'I am not your brother to be watched with impunity,' he responded, calmly. 'But I'm sure the Armstrongs will be interested in your opinion.'

'The Armstrongs?' I did not understand.

'You are shouting,' Hugh explained. 'Your voice will carry right across the Moss.'

He was right of course, damn the man. I sat down again in the shelter of the jagged teeth of the Wolf Craigs and glared across at him instead. Unfortunately, he did not seem in the slightest put out by even my most ferocious frown. Presumably, his sisters had similar tricks. Damn that man. Damn him for the devilry of the Veitches.

'You had best get some sleep,' Hugh said mildly. 'We have a hard night ahead of us.'

'We have just had a hard night.' I was not quite prepared for a reconciliation.

'Tomorrow we skirt Liddesdale,' he said.

That name sent a chill through me, as well it might. I have mentioned Liddesdale before, as anybody talking of the old Border must. It was the worst valley in the Borderland and therefore perhaps the most dangerous place in the whole of Europe. Even royal armies walked wary when passing through, and although the King had a garrison there in Hermitage Castle, that place had its own reputation of cruelty and menace. You will have heard of robber barons? Well in Liddesdale, every baron was a robber and every family a riding family; you will know that in our Border the name riding and raiding were synonymous. A riding family was one that struck out by night or day to reive or rob the cattle and goods from others, be they ten miles away or a hundred and ten. Every night from autumn to spring the hills were busy with reiving bands that could be three strong or three thousand.

Liddesdale was home to the most dangerous of these families and we had to pass it to get home. I did not sleep well that day as we lay between the red fangs of the wolf with the air damp above and the ground hard beneath. Hugh scooped a hold to cup my hip, which helped and twice during the day I stirred, to see him on watch. He looked down on me, put a finger to his lips and winked.

I woke with his jack covering me, a pounding head, and the knowledge that we had a bad night ahead augmented by the tension between us. I handed him back his jack without a word. I did not know how to thank him that day.

'Are you ready?' Standing at the side of the Wolf Craigs with the sun setting behind him, Hugh's face was hidden. I saw him in silhouette with his broad shoulders, trim waist, and the flare of his hips leading to long straight legs.

'You look like some sort of Greek God,' I said and immediately regretted my words as he turned away.

'That was meant to be a compliment,' I added.

'I know it was,' he said shortly. 'Mount Kailzie and ride.'

I mounted Kailzie and I rode, wishing I had never opened my mouth or tried friendship with this moody, capable, complex man. The Moss looked exactly the same as it had the previous night, dark and damp, with patches of mist drifting around the peat-bogs and twisted trees like the ghosts of the damned, leaking leaves to a fluky wind.

'Look.' Hugh pointed ahead. I saw what looked like a small copse of trees with firelight flickering at their side. 'A watch fire. The Armstrongs have posted men there.' He studied the fire, slowly counting. 'I see five men.'

'Can't we go round?' I asked.

In reply, he took me by the hand and helped me, quite gently from the back of my horse. He led me ten steps to the right. 'Stop there,' he said, 'and stretch out one foot.'

I did so. The mud sucked at me so fiercely I thought I might lose my boot. I withdrew quickly, with Hugh holding me.

'There is a stretch of black bog like that all the way around this damnable moss,' Hugh said, 'mile upon mile of it, except for three places, the three yetts, or gates of Tarras. This is the Black Yett, the least known of them. We can drown in the bog or face the Armstrongs.'

I was silent for a space. 'What do we do?'

'I need you to keep your tongue under control and do exactly as I say.' Hugh had his answer ready. 'Can you do that?'

'I don't know about my tongue…' I began and stopped myself. 'Yes,' I said. 'Yes, I can do that.'

'Good.' He helped me back on Kailzie, where the renewed pressure pushed into my tender parts. I did not protest. 'Now hold on and trust me.' Walking in front, he led me a full fifty paces into the dark to one of the wind-twisted Scots Pines. 'Stand here,' he said, 'and the tree will shield your shape. The wind is coming from the west so it will drive your scent away from the track.'

I nodded, obeying his instructions not to speak.

'I will distract the Armstrongs long enough for them to leave the yett unguarded. They will ride past you into the Moss. I want you to wait until all five have passed and then you will come out and ride through the yett as if all the devils of hell were sticking red hot pokers into your…' he stopped as I concealed my smile. Hugh had nearly dropped his guard then and I liked him all the more for it. 'When all five have passed I want you to ride as fast as you can through the yett. There is a small slope on the other side. Go down the slope and turn right. Ride straight and true until you come to a ruined chapel. Wait for me there. Have you got that?'

'I have got that,' I said.

'If I am not there within two hours then I am not coming,' Hugh continued. 'In that case, you must wait for dark tomorrow and ride northward; follow the Pole Star.'

'Why would you not come?' I asked in a small voice.

'Because I will be dead,' Hugh said.

'What?' But I spoke to myself. Hugh had vanished into the dark as if he had never been there. I sat on Kailzie beside that gnarled pine with the ache of loneliness in my heart and fear in my soul. 'But I don't want you dead,' I said softly, 'I want you with me.' Nobody heard except the wind, and the wind does not care what we want. It follows its own course, whatever that happens to be. And anyway, Hugh was not my man; Robert was my man and he would be out there somewhere, scouring the hills for me.

I could see the flicker of firelight by the darker patch that I knew to be woodland, and I could smell the occasional whiff of smoke, sweet and pleasant in the night air. It was a few long minutes before I heard a long drawn out call, like the scream of a hunting vixen, and the words 'A Veitch! A Veitch!'

That was Hugh. There was no other Veitch in the area and nobody else would beard the Armstrongs in their own Tarras Moss. I heard the clash of steel on steel and then the sound of galloping hooves as one horseman thundered past me. A few seconds later came the shout 'A Veitch! A Veitch!' once again, and then more horsemen and the cry, 'An Armstrong!' Long drawn out and echoing to the silent sky.

Tempted to charge in their wake and help Hugh, I knew that I would be more hindrance than help and instead pushed Kailzie forward and toward the Black Yett. I was nervous for Hugh and apprehensive in case the Armstrongs had left a man behind. I should not have bothered; the only man there lay on his back, arms outstretched. He may have been dead, he may have been alive, I did not know. I passed him with a scared glance and trotted on, hoping that Hugh was safe in the Moss as I tried to remember my instructions.

The Black Yett was ill marked by two large stones like the ones the ancient Druids used for worship, or so I have been told, and beyond there was a slope, just as Hugh had said. We slithered down, Kailzie and I, and I nearly dismounted myself in my haste. There was grass at the foot, sweet and fresh despite the lateness of the season, and I thought: was it left, or right?

It was right, I was sure it was right, so I pulled Kailzie in that direction and kicked in my heels to cover the ground at a faster rate. We had not travelled more than half a mile when I saw the shell of a building that could only be the chapel, although only God knew why anybody would wish to build a chapel in such a forlorn spot.

Somebody told me that this had once been a spital, a hospital, a stopping off spot for travellers traversing the lonely road between the great abbeys of the Scottish Border and the towns of England, and that may well be true. All I saw was a small, stone building with a pointed gable pierced with a round window. I led Kailzie inside this ruined sanctuary and let her graze because God knew she had been hard-worked on short rations the last few days. I was getting rather fond of that brown mare.

I was also getting rather fond of Hugh, moody and unpredictable though he was. I leaned against the cold, moss-furred stone walls of that ancient building, listened to the wind and waited. And waited. Border bred, I did not normally feel the cold but as I stood there a chill seemed to creep over me. It may have emanated from the ground or from the worn stones with whatever history they had, I do not know. I only know that within a short space of time I was shivering, pulling my clothes up to cover me, and hoping that Hugh came along soon. I began seeing and hearing things in the dark, imagining that the rustle of bracken in a crack in the wall was an Armstrong coming to get me, or the distant bark of a fox was a horseman nosing in with drawn sword and evil intent. I began to form people out of shadows, such was the state of my imagination, so that a shift of moonlight cast the very image of Wild Will walking toward me, and the glint of a star on a burn became the ripple of light along the blade of a broadsword. I pulled my shawl closer about me and gasped with shock as a voice broke the silence.

'You did well, Jeannie.'

'Hugh?' I peered into the dark, half fearful in case it was an Armstrong or the Redcap demon from Hermitage Castle only a few miles away.

'Hugh it is.' He stepped into a circle of moonlight, looking taller than I remembered from only an hour or two ago.

'The Armstrongs?'

'They won't be bothering us,' he assured me. 'I have a gift for you out here.'

I followed him outside the walls of the chapel, part expecting to see the head of a dead Armstrong or some such thing. As children, Robert and I had scared each other with such tales. When faced with the reality there was no pleasure; only the fear was real.

'Here.' Hugh lifted a spare saddle from the back of his horse. 'One each. The previous owners have no further use for them.'

I did not ask further. I only held the saddle closely. 'You have no idea how much a certain part of me is grateful for this gift.'

Hugh leaned closer. 'I understand,' he said. 'Certain parts of me are equally grateful.' His smile was mischievous. I did not mention the smear of blood across his face. I knew that it was not his.

'You are a good man,' I said, and he turned away. I cursed myself for my wayward tongue.

'We had better keep moving,' Hugh said, 'I'd like as much distance as possible between us and the Black Yett.'

Having a saddle under me was infinitely more comfortable than riding without, so riding was much less of a hardship than it had been. The ground was also easier, springy turf and soft heather with less need to watch for peat-holes, bogland, and sudden patches of dense forest. I began to feel quite relaxed until we crested a ridge and Hugh put a hand on the bridle of my horse.

'Wait now,' he said softly and gestured beneath us.

The ridge stretched into the unseen dark and on its north it overlooked Liddesdale. Below us, deep in degradation and specked by flickering lights from fireside and window, swept that dreaded valley. Even up here with the fresh night wind blowing and the occasional spatter of rain cleaning the air, I could sense the wickedness.

'We have a choice,' Hugh said. 'We can either go around the valley, which means a ride of around forty miles or more, or we can cross it, which is much more dangerous and very much shorter.'

'Which shall we do?' I asked.

'We must decide between us,' Hugh said.

I looked at him. Nobody had ever asked my opinion about such matters before. In the Lethan, Father made all the decisions about farming or anything outside Cardrona Tower, while Mother was the matriarch of all within. There was no argument. Here, Hugh was treating me as if I mattered, as if I was important. It was a new sensation. 'Thank you,' I said simply.

'Thank you for what?' He sounded genuinely curious.

'For asking me,' I said. 'Not many men would have done so.'

He looked away. 'It is your life as much as mine,' Hugh said.

I pondered the choices; the longer, safer ride meant at least another night out in the open, another night on the hills that bordered the Armstrong homeland. It also meant another night of worry for my parents. And for Robert of course. How on earth could I forget my own Robert? On the other hand, if we crossed directly…

'How long would it take to cross the valley?' I asked.

'That depends on luck,' Hugh said. 'Liddesdale is not a single valley; it is Y-shaped. If we manage to cross the downstroke of the Y we could be over in three hours at the most. If we are less lucky it will take twice as long, or we could be there forever, mouldering at the foot of a shallow grave.'

'Let's try it,' I said. 'If you agree.' I felt a surge of excitement at the thought of crossing the Armstrong homeland of Liddesdale. Until the Yorling's raid, I had never thought of the Armstrongs except as a distant menace. Although we were always prepared for a raid on the Lethan, I had not considered Liddesdale or the Armstrongs as being a direct threat to me. Now, since I had met Wild Will face to scarred face and I knew what sort of man he was, I detested him and the whole Armstrong clan. They were my enemy and I wished to show them my contempt. I wanted to cross their damned valley to prove I was not scared.

Which, surprisingly, I was not. Why I was not scared, I did not know as Wild Will was undoubtedly the most dangerous man I had ever met.

'We will be passing through the most feared valley in the country,' Hugh reminded me.

'I know,' I said, 'but you will take care of me.' Once again, I had spoken before I thought.

'I am glad you think so.' I was surprised that Hugh replied so quickly. I was no longer surprised that he did not look at me. I knew I had embarrassed him again. Why did I keep doing that to a man who had shown me nothing but kindness and help?

'Dismount,' he ordered and lent me his hand to help me down. I watched as he took a padded jack from behind his saddle, cut it into strips and wrapped them around Kailzie's hooves.

'What are you doing?' I asked.

'Muffling any sound,' he said, moving across to his own horse to do the same. 'Now keep behind me and keep very quiet.'

I took a deep breath, wondered if I had made the correct choice in venturing into Liddesdale, and followed. We padded downhill, following a sheep track that seemed to favour the steepest parts of the incline. I kept my eye on the shadowy shape of Hugh as he negotiated the hillside, passing from the steep upper slopes to the sides of the tilled ridges, whose crops were not yet gathered despite the lateness of the season. No doubt the men of Liddesdale had more important things to do than gather their crops, such as abducting stray women.

Somewhere a dog barked, the sound waking others, so their sharp yapping echoed through the night. By now I knew to stop at any sounds: we were less visible motionless. Harsh shouts quietened the dogs. Silence returned, cracked only by the faint lowing of cattle and the rustle of sheep moving in the outfields. We moved on, slowly, cautiously, two hunted people moving across the realm of the hunter, the prey passing the den of the lion, the mouse thumbing his nose at the home of the cat. And my bottom still ached damnably, despite my fancy new saddle.

There were many more habitations along the valley floor and on the lower hill slopes than I had expected. Most were small, little more than huts, cottages with drystone walls and roofs of heather-thatch, with the dung piles and peat stacks outside.

'Wait.' Hugh hissed the words and pulled my horse into the shadow of a farmstead. I heard the hoof beats a moment later and watched as a body of horsemen passed us, driving a small herd of ragged cattle. I knew they had been reiving, possibly across the Border in England, or up in Teviotdale. They moved silently, professional thieves engaged in their lawless business. That was what Liddesdale was infamous for; that was how these people lived.

We waited until the reivers were passed and moved on. I felt slightly sick, with my heart pounding and my mouth dry, yet I knew that, despite my fear, I would not have missed this for all the world. I was living, I was out in the world, sharing experiences with a vibrant man and I would relive these days again and again in the years to come. I would tell my children and grandchildren of the time that Hugh Veitch and I crossed the Tarras Moss and Liddesdale despite every effort of the Armstrongs to capture us.

If I lived of course.

And if we had grandchildren, Robert and I.

The Liddel Water ran down the centre of the valley. Swollen with autumnal rains, it was fast and deep and dark and dangerous. I hesitated at the approach until Hugh took hold of Kailzie's bridle and led the way, easing his horse into the water. I heard the rattle of hooves against loose stones, felt Kailzie shudder as she slipped on the greasy bottom and gasped as Hugh guided me over. There was a single moment of doubt as we mounted the northern bank and then both horses were on dry land, legs and underbellies dripping and the worst of Liddesdale behind us. I allowed myself to breathe again and gave Hugh a broad smile. He lifted a hand in response as he glanced around him, his eyes wary and mobile.

There were lights ahead, a small group of houses set within a stone wall, the dark shape of a rowan tree placed to ward off witches and a squat peel tower. I swear I saw the silhouette of a man on the roof with a steel morion on his head and a spear balanced over his shoulder.

'We have to pass that,' Hugh said softly. 'It is the only route.'

I nodded, feeling the thrill of increased danger. Hugh would get us through; I had faith in him like I had in no other man. I closed my eyes, knowing that I should not think that. I was being disloyal to Robert and disloyalty was the worst of all crimes in the Border litany. Theft, robbery, reiving, assault, hamesucken, even murder was allowed, but loyalty was paramount. Loyalty to the surname, the valley, and the husband or wife was what mattered.

It was my wandering thoughts that caused the trouble. Kailzie had a mind of her own; she sensed my lapse of concentration and decided to go her own way rather than mine; a hay stall outside the peel tower proved more attractive than my desires and the horse pulled to the side. Taken by surprise I hauled on the reins, Kailzie voiced her objection with a loud neigh and a stamping of her hind legs and the sound carried in the night.

'Who's that?' the watchman called from atop the tower roof. 'State your business in the Liddel Peel!'

I did not need Hugh to warn me to keep quiet. Suddenly, all the excitement and drama of the night had vanished, and pure naked fear had taken its place. I felt one of Hugh's hard hands clamp over my mouth as the other took hold of Kailzie's reins.

We stopped, standing still in the slight shadow of the peel tower with the sinister slither of the Liddle Water a spear's throw behind us and the rising slopes of the hills inviting escape to the north.

'State your name and business!' That harsh voice sounded again, and then came the insistent clamour of a warning bell as the sentry shouted a warning.

'To arms Liddel Peel! Intruders at the gate!'

'Run!' Hugh released my mouth and reins. 'Gallop for your life and don't stop for anything!'

I heard the clatter of feet from within the gaunt tower, heard men shouting and the clash of equipment and I kicked in my spurs and headed for the high hills. Before I had ridden fifty yards the great door of Liddle Peel was open, and a deluge of horsemen clattered out. I had time for one single glance behind me and saw a sight that I knew would haunt me for the remainder of my life, however short that time may be.

There were a round dozen men emerging from the peel tower, some fully accoutred with helmet, jack and lance, others less well equipped. One wore only a pair of long white drawers and held a naked sword high, while his long hair streamed behind him like a plume. Another rode stark naked, a lithe young hero with his mouth open in a challenge and a lance couched ready to kill. Him I would have taken time to examine if I was not so scared, I could hardly think. There was a pair of old grey-beards, men of wisdom and undoubted wickedness who had probably seen a hundred skirmishes and battles, and a bevvy of youngsters who could not yet have reached their teens, all intent on catching us and spitting us clean on sword and lance.

With that one glance confirming our danger, I put spur to horse and fled. I saw Hugh in front, his face anxious as he looked over his shoulder to ensure my safety, and I saw the fields rising in front to the welcome greyness of the surrounding hills and the comforting shield of night.

'Stay close,' Hugh shouted urgently.

I spurred urgently, feeling sorry for Kailzic, feeling scared for myself and Hugh. I felt less sorry for Kailzie when she bucked under the prick of my spurs, nearly throwing me. I held on grimly, very aware of the horsemen clattering through the dark behind me.

Liddesdale was awake. All along the valley as far as I could see lights were coming on as householders put fire to torches or stoked up their fires and opened their doors. Horsemen were gathering as well as masses of men on foot, while children and women were shouting to one another the length and breadth of the valley.

The Tweedie Passion

'Jeannie!' Hugh's shout was urgent. He reined up beside me, grabbed hold of my bridle and pulled me away to the left. 'They're in front of us.'

Peering into the dark I saw shadowy shapes, heard the rattle of bridles and stirrup, and followed Hugh off the path and back down to the valley floor, following the bank of the Liddel Water. I hoped there were no men ahead; I had chosen badly when I wanted to cross this valley. My vanity had proved costly. We looked for a gap to the north, some path or opening that would allow us access to the long bald hills in which we could hide, and which would eventually take us home to Peebles-shire and the Lethan Valley. Instead, all we saw were armed men, riding to block our path, chanting their slogans 'An Armstrong, an Armstrong' or 'An Elliot', 'A Nixon' or whatever riding family to which they claimed their allegiance.

'All Liddesdale is up!' I shouted.

'This way!' Hugh's grin took me by surprise. Trapped in the middle of Liddesdale, surrounded by hundreds of some of the wildest riders in Europe, in the middle of the night and with a woman to look after, he gave me a wide, cheerful grin. 'Let's confuse the Armstrongs.'

Raising his voice to a roar, he shouted 'An Armstrong! An Armstrong!' as loudly as he could and led me back over the Liddel that we had crossed with such hope only a few moments before. I followed, feeling my heart sink yet trusting Hugh with all that I had. Or nearly all that I had. One precious thing I still reserved for Robert, but at that moment I had no thought for that part of me and every thought for saving all the rest.

In the dark, it was hard to differentiate between friend and foe, and now that we were riding in the same direction as everybody else, and shouting the same slogan, there was less attention paid to us. 'They're at the Castleton!' Hugh yelled. 'It's a raid by the Grahams!'

His words, shouted with authority and roared out in the dark, had some effect. Many of the riders headed south and west down the flow of the Liddel. Others did not. Stray voices gave contradictory orders.

'This is Mangerton!' The voice roared from this side of the Liddel. I knew that Armstrong of Mangerton was one of the chiefs of the Armstrongs so his name carried more authority than any anonymous voice in the dark. 'Light the bale fires! Form patrols!'

'That's not so good,' Hugh did not lose his smile. 'They will be all around the valley in minutes. We have to hide inside Liddesdale.' I could nearly hear his mind working. 'Are you superstitious?'

The question took me by surprise. 'What?' I am sure I stared blankly at him.

'Are you superstitious? Are you scared of ghosts and bogles and demons?' He glanced around, lifting his hand to wave to a passing group of Croziers as if he knew them well. 'I know that you are well used to dragons!'

Was this a time to joke? Obviously, Hugh thought so, to judge by his smile.

'Well, are you superstitious?'

I shook my head. 'No more than anybody else,' I said. I remembered the childhood stories that Robert and I had shared when we tried to frighten each other with tales of witches and fairies. My stories had always been more vivid than his, so that on more than one occasion he had held my hand as we ran home through the dark valley to Whitecleuch or Cardona Tower.

'Good: come with me then.'

We changed direction for the third time that night. Rather than trying to escape across the valley or joining the men who rode purposefully to their designated positions, he led me up the valley to a spur that lifted some thousand feet high. Hugh had mentioned that the Liddel Valley formed a Y shape if you remember? Well, we were now ascending the fork of the Y, the crotch, if I may be so crude.

'Not many people come up here.' Hugh was a bit breathless as he forced his horse up the steep slope. 'It's haunted, you see. Even the Armstrongs are afraid of ghosts.'

'Are you sure it's the ghosts that daunt them and not the climb?' I pushed poor Kailzie as hard as the mare could go as we ascended that slithering, slippery slope.

We stopped eventually with our horses breathing hard and my muscles aching with strain. Hugh dismounted and helped me off Kailzie. I thought his hand lingered a fraction too long on my arm, but I may have been mistaken. I know I thrust out my bottom slightly too much as I swung off the horse. I did not mean to; it was some instinct over which I had no control. I do know that he took no notice, the pig.

'Where are we?' In the dark, I could not see much except a number of humped shapes that could have been tree stumps, ruined dwellings, or perhaps great rocks. 'Are we safe here?'

'We'll have to stay here for the day and try and get away tomorrow night,' Hugh said. 'They call this the Nine Stane Rig.'

I knew the name and the evil reputation. Suddenly I felt a chill descend. 'I know the story,' I said.

'All of it?' Hugh's voice was quiet. 'This is a stone circle with nine great standing stones, used by the ancients, maybe the Druids for human sacrifice, they say.'

'I have heard that,' I said, 'although I have never been here before.'

'Not many have,' Hugh told me. 'Not even the Armstrongs come here. That is why I asked if you were scared of bogles and demons and such like.'

'I have never met one,' I controlled the tremor in my voice, 'and have had no reason to fear them.'

'I will tell you the story,' Hugh said, 'once we are settled in.' He did the usual, knee haltering the horses and checking the ground for the best place to lie concealed. We found ourselves in the very centre of the circle, with the ancient stones all around us, chilling in their knowledge.

'Lie still,' Hugh ordered me. 'I will be back shortly.'

'Where are you going?' But he was already gone, slipping into the night. As always when he disappeared, I felt lonely, as if something good had vanished from my life. I was beginning to depend on that man too much. Indeed, I was also beginning to like him far too much and I knew I could not allow that.

I lay there, wondering where he was and what he was doing. I also wondered about Robert and my parents. They must be missing me. The thought of their familiar faces and my chamber in Cardrona Tower nearly brought tears. I knew I had to be strong to survive this ordeal: I could not allow myself to weaken.

Unable to lie still, I stood up and walked around inside the circle of stones. Now, what I am about to relate next, you may not believe and you may not understand. Well, neither do I. It happened and that is the end of it. Please remember though, that I was born on the midnight of Midsummer's Day, so I am perhaps more susceptible to these sorts of events.

It was not dramatic. One minute I was leaning against the nearest of the stones, looking down the valley in the hope of seeing Hugh return, and then a vision came. It was not my usual vision of the burning tower and the scar-faced man. It was a far different one, where I was older, sitting in a chair in a comfortable chamber with a bright fire sparkling within a broad fireplace and tapestries hanging on the wall. I was in an armed chair, with a baby in my arms and a child playing around my feet. I knew I was at home, wherever that home happened to be.

There was a man walking away from me, laughing as he carried a third child. He was tall and broad and confident yet, with his back turned, I could not see his face. I wanted desperately to see this man that I knew to be my husband. I longed for him to turn. Only when he opened the door did I see the coat of arms on the wall above. I looked up, noting the device and the name beneath. The first words were blurred but the first part of the last was clear. It read Robert. I lifted the baby to my shoulder to rub his back and break his wind and rose to read the rest of the name.

'Jeannie?' Hugh was handing something to me. I was back on the Nine Stane Rig with the usual rain descending and the stones pointing to a weeping sky. 'Eat.'

It was a leg of chicken, still warm from somebody's fireside. 'Where did this come from?'

'With most of the people rushing about looking for intruders, nobody is minding their own houses.' Hugh was quite calm. 'I have quite a bag of spoil: apples, chicken, beef, a new cloak for you, two kerchiefs, clean underwear, a kirtle, and sleeves... all courtesy of our kindly hosts, the Armstrongs.'

I grabbed at this gift from heaven. Unless you have spent days astride a horse crossing scores of miles of wild territory without a change of clothes, you have no idea how luxurious such a simple thing as clean underwear can be. I had been concerned about that important little matter for quite some time. 'I could kiss you for that,' I said as once again my mouth captured my thoughts and broadcast them without consideration.

'There will be no need for the kissing,' Hugh said, turning away.

I closed my eyes, wondering how many ways I could embarrass this man before he decided that I was not worth his bother.

'You are a kind man,' I said stoutly, 'and nobody could disagree with that.'

'The previous owner of these articles could disagree,' Hugh said.

I frowned at that. You see, in our Border, we accepted reiving as part of life. Thieving the property of a rival family, especially one with whom we had a feud, was accepted as normal. There was no stigma attached. The Armstrongs were hunting us down; therefore, they were fair game for us to rob.

'Hugh,' I said. 'It was my fault that the valley woke.'

He screwed his face up so it looked even uglier yet strangely more attractive. 'It happened,' he said.

'Yes; and it was my fault that it happened.' If I had been so inattentive with Father or Mother, they would not have been backward in telling me exactly how foolish I was. Robert too would have been withering in his scorn; I expected Hugh to launch a vicious tirade against me. Instead, he merely touched me on the shoulder.

'We are safe now,' he said.

'Thank you,' I said simply, although I doubt he knew for what I was thanking him.

He smiled. 'Now.' He put down another bag as he sat beside me, leaning against the standing stone. 'I was telling you the story of this circle.'

That was the end of it. He never mentioned that incident again.

'In the old days, a man named De Soulis was the Lord of Liddesdale and Captain of Hermitage Castle.' Hugh's deep voice filled the space between the standing stones yet was so low it would not have penetrated beyond. 'He had the reputation of being a bad, wicked man and that was confirmed when the people discovered him stealing the local children to use for his black magic. The people of the valley, the ancestors of the Armstrongs, Elliots, and the rest, decided to take their revenge. They took the evil Lord Soulis to this stone circle,' Hugh waved a casual hand around him, 'wrapped him in lead and popped him in a cauldron.'

'And quite right too,' I approved. 'That is what happens to evil men.'

'Oh, there is more,' Hugh said. 'They popped him in a cauldron, lit a fire underneath and boiled him into soup, which they then drank.'

I stared around me. For one fleeting instant, I saw the men and women of Liddesdale wrestling Lord Soulis into a cauldron and boiling it up. I could hear his screeches as he boiled to death, and I could see the people crowded round, laughing at their revenge as they drank the Soulis soup.

'That is horrible,' I said.

'They say that on dark nights people with the gift can see the people boiling Lord Soulis and can hear his death screams.'

'What nonsense,' I scoffed, looking fearfully into the night.

'I hope you don't get nightmares,' Hugh said.

'Not with you here,' I said quickly and looked away before he did.

It was a few moments before Hugh spoke again. 'I know it is wet,' he said, 'but try and get some sleep. We are moving just before dawn.'

'We're riding in daylight?' I looked up in disbelief.

'The Armstrongs are not fools.' Hugh was no longer smiling. 'They know that any fugitive will sit tight during the day and ride at night. Sooner or later somebody will see our hoof prints leading up here and they will work out where we are. The best thing we can do is hide where they will not expect to see us. We will hide in the open.'

'I don't understand,' I said.

'We are going to ride right through the middle of Liddesdale as though we own the place,' Hugh told me. 'Slow and brazen.' His grin was now as broad as I had ever seen it. 'And that will be a story you can tell your grandchildren!'

I felt that renewed surge of mingled excitement and anticipation as I contemplated riding through Liddesdale. That vision returned, with my husband, if it was my husband, and the three children, with the word Robert on the coat of arms. 'You are a daring man,' I said.

'I am just a man,' Hugh replied.

This time I did not allow him to back away. 'No, Hugh,' I said. 'You are a man of daring. In truth, I have never met a man like you before.'

Hugh frowned. 'There is nothing special about me...'

I took hold of his arm, unsure how I felt. I know I was angry but there were other emotions there also, some of them that I did not want to admit. 'There is a lot special about you.'

He pulled his way clear, not as gently as I would have liked. I took hold of him; determined not to let him go. 'Hugh,' I said, 'I am paying you a compliment.'

'I know you are!' Hugh did not attempt to free himself.

'Then allow me to say nice things about you!' I stood up, holding him by the forearm. It was as hard as iron and so thick I could hardly span it with both hands. 'You have saved me in a dozen different situations. Every day you do something that surprises me, from not spying on me when I am washing, to bringing me new clothes or not blaming me when I nearly got us both killed.' I was talking quickly now, not sure what I expected to happen but certain that I intended something.

Hugh eased his arm away. 'You freed me first,' he said.

'You saved me second, and third, and fourth, and fifth.' I stood back. The standing stone was hard at my back. I thought I could feel some power surging through it, some elemental force that I could not understand. Or perhaps the power came from me and I transmitted it to the stone. I do not know. I only know that I was very aware of some sensation that I had never known before.

'You are the gentlest man I have ever met,' I told him.

'A gentle man who kills people.' Hugh took another step away from me.

'Don't you like compliments?' I asked him. 'Don't you like people being nice to you?' I lowered my voice, lest half the outlaws of Liddesdale heard us and climbed up to listen to a conversation that I suspected was about to become quite heated. I stepped closer and raised my face to his to emphasise my point.

'No,' Hugh said softly. 'No, I don't.'

'Why not?' I finally lost my temper with this frustrating, lovely, capable, maddening non-ugly man. 'Why don't you like me complimenting you, damn it?'

'Because, dear sweet Jeannie,' he obviously kept his own temper with something of an effort, 'I have fallen in love with you.'

'Oh.' I stepped back again. 'Oh.' I did not take my gaze off his face. That was the last thing I had expected to hear.

'And you have your Robert,' Hugh said. 'You do not want me.'

Did I not want him? I touched the stone once more. Did I want him? I felt that same sensation surging through me again and I searched inside myself. I thought of Robert and how we had promised ourselves to each other many years ago and had remained faithful ever since. I thought of the years we had spent growing up, the experiences we had shared in childhood and youth. I remembered the promises we had made to each other and which we had renewed year after year, making rings of grass and twining them around our childish fingers as tokens of our love.

And then I looked up at Hugh as he stood beside me with his uncertain, rugged face and all the past washed away in a flood of recent memories and feelings. I thought of his constant care, his capability and, perhaps most of all, of that half hour or so when I had stood behind a tree and watched him at the waterfall.

'Yes, I do,' I said, so softly that I hardly heard my own voice. 'Oh yes, I do want you.'

Suddenly that wanting exploded inside me. It had lain dormant, waiting its opportunity since those first few minutes in the dungeon when I heard Hugh's voice. Now it was like a torrent of desire. My mother had warned me of the Tweedie Passion that lay volcanic within everybody of our name, and now I had my first experience that I was not immune. I was a Tweedie, with my full measure of the Tweedie Passion.

Hugh turned slowly toward me, with that ugly-handsome face sharing my torment. Ignoring the rain, I peeled off the outer layer of my clothing as I stepped toward him. 'Hugh,' I said, and put my hands on his face. He was rough-skinned, a day unshaven so the bristles rasped against my palms: the feel of a man.

'Jeannie...' I heard the tension in his voice and saw the shadows flitting across those normally-steady eyes.

I kissed him, full on the mouth. One soft, lingering kiss with my mouth closed as I pressed my lips against his.

He pulled back with his eyes wild and his breathing ragged. 'Jeannie...'

I do not know what he was going to say. I did not want to know what he was going to say. It was not a time for words. The Tweedie Passion was upon me, urging me on, forcing me to act. I suddenly had no wish to control my actions; I acted out of instinct. Stepping back, I stripped off my clothes as we stood there within the circle of ancient stones, releasing my hair so it flowed dark as my own midnight around my shoulders and down my back, so the end kissed the upper curves of my buttocks in a faint hint of the pleasures I wanted.

The expression of Hugh's eyes altered. The shadows merged together so his eyes darkened, the pupils dilating until they dominated. His breathing became as ragged as my own as he reached out for me.

His hands caressed, cupping my face and moving down to my shoulders, smoothing my skin, and then he slid them down to my breasts. His breathing roughened more until he was almost panting.

My hands were shaking as I reached forward, unfastening the ties of his jack, pulling it from his chest and stomach, dropping it heedlessly on the ground. His shirt was next, the stiff linen no obstacle as I hauled it over his head, so his face emerged, tousle-haired, ready for my next kiss.

The Passion took over my tongue as I thrust it within his mouth in untutored lust. His teeth were even, his own tongue eager to meet me, his chest hard against my breasts, his stomach cobbled with muscles as we pressed against each other, man to woman and woman to man, each equal in passion and desire.

Untaught, I gyrated my hips, pressing hard, feeling the swell and bulge of his manhood against me as I swept my hands down his shoulders and over his back and around the swell of his hips, to urgently unfasten his breeches. I eased them down, manoeuvred them less than carefully over the essential part of him and allowed them to drop around his ankles.

His buttocks were taut and hard as marble with skin surprisingly smooth. I dug my fingers in and pulled him to me, feeling his desire eager against me.

We sunk to the ground together, uncaring of the dangers all around us. His mouth sought mine, his hands were on my bottom, caressing, fingers gentle yet urgent, my legs apart, opening, welcoming him within as his mouth dipped, his teeth nibbled at the breasts that I proffered for his attention.

There was a moment of welcome pain as he penetrated me and I felt him within, warm and welcome as my body took control. The Tweedie Passion had me in its grasp and there was nothing I could do to resist. I had no thoughts of Robert or of anybody else. Only salacity, desire, carnality, fervour; call it anything you wish, but you cannot capture the urgency with which I embraced that, my first taste of love. I knew it was wrong; I knew that I was breaking my decade-long promise to Robert and I cared not the fraction of a whit.

At that moment, I wanted Hugh's body more than anything else and I would have my desire whatever the church, God, Mother, or the Laws and customs of the Border ordained. Something was in control that was far more fundamental than any man-made or God-ordained stricture, something over which I had as much control as I had over the passage of the Moon or the ordering of the tides. It was the nature of Woman, the eternal search for reproduction and the lust for a man: it was the Tweedie Passion that controlled me and at that moment I was utterly determined to enjoy every last second of what I was doing and to hang with the consequences.

I lay on my back as he thrust within me. I rose to meet each movement of his hips, my hands on his buttocks, nails digging deep, demanding more and more, and he met each demand with skill and energy. Then I was astride him, laughing, shrieking with joy as my hair descended to his face like a damp curtain over which the rain wept tears of pleasure. His face was mine; his body was mine; his pleasure was mine as I was his as we united in a union surely blessed by the Gods of Love or at least the Gods of Passion.

I explored him with my mouth as he did the same to me, probing every curve and cavity, every indentation and protuberance with tongue and hand and lips and nothing but joy and intense stimulation as the rain failed to cool our desire and the circle of ancient standing stones retained our energy, enhanced it and watched silently as we lost ourselves to everything but sensual pleasure; or perhaps to love.

Until all energy was spent, and we lay there, side by side on the rough, damp grass, watching each other as the sweet madness eased and the panting slowed with the hammer of our hearts.

And sanity returned together with a realisation of the awful, incredible things that we had done.

'Oh, dear God,' I said softly as I sat up, belatedly trying to cover all that I had revealed with such abandoned glee.

'Oh, Jeannie…' Hugh stared at me. 'Oh, Jeannie: I should not have…'

We stared at each other. Now I knew what Mother had meant by a full woman and now I knew what she meant by a full man. I was a woman now; no longer a girl and Hugh was undoubtedly a man. Of that, I had incontrovertible proof.

'I have broken my oath.' I backed away in a half crouch, covering my womanhood as if that would help. 'I have betrayed my trust.' For a second, I hated Hugh and sought ways of blaming him for what had happened. I knew that was unfair and wrong. The fault was not with Hugh. The fault was with me, with the Tweedie Passion.

Hugh did not cover himself. He stood naked in the rain, looking at me through those very clear eyes. 'I allowed this to happen,' he said. 'You are in no way to blame.' He bent down, unsheathed his sword, reversed it, and handed me the handle. He placed the point against his chest, directly in line with his heart. 'If you believe I have wronged you, then I invite you to press the blade home.'

Still as bare as any new-born baby, I took hold of the handle. It was rough in my fist, with the yard-long blade heavy. I held Hugh's life in my hand, and he was a willing participant. Life or death; I had the power. I pressed slightly, holding his gaze as the point of his sword bit into his skin.

'Push if you will.' Hugh did not flinch as a tiny drop of blood appeared at the tip of the sword. Rainwater diluted it to a pinkish fluid that dribbled down the blade, spreading out as it neared the guard. 'I have only one thing to add. I regret any insult or damage I have said or done to you. I do not regret what happened between us. It was a sweet, joyous experience that I will remember for the rest of my life, whether that be one minute or one hundred years.'

I could not press the point home: I had no desire to take revenge on Hugh.

I dropped the sword with a clatter.

'I cannot kill you, Hugh,' I said, wiping away the blood that seeped down his chest.

'If your Robert seeks retribution,' Hugh said, 'I will meet him willingly, wherever and however he wishes.'

I took a single step back. The sky was beginning to lighten with the promised onset of dawn. I could see the circle of stones plainly now, thrusting their message of mystery to the mourning clouds above. I would fain have blamed them for my weakness and forgotten this whole sorry episode if I could, but I knew my own hot blood had been the cause. I could not escape that. Nor could I escape my feelings.

I looked across at this naked man.

'Hugh,' I said quietly. 'It was equally as joyous and sweet for me.'

'Oh...' His mouth dropped open. I think that was the first time I had surprised him. 'Now I think it best that we get our clothes on, don't you?' I forced a smile that I hoped was sweet. 'I for one am getting cold standing here in the rain, and if we are to get up this cursed valley we should move soon.'

He nodded, once, and put out his hand, but dropped it before he touched me. 'Let us get on then,' he said, with his gaze not faltering. He stooped to lift his sword and slid it into the scabbard with an audible hiss. 'If things were different between us,' he said, 'I would not be walking away from you.'

I watched him dress, with my eyes savouring every movement of his body and limbs. Despite my guilt, I could not control my feelings and had no desire to do so.

'Put this on, Jeannie.' Hugh opened the second bag he had brought with him and passed over a pair of male breeches and a protective jack. 'A woman riding astride will attract attention wherever she goes. A young man dressed like everybody else will hardly merit a glance.'

'Thank you.' I had never worn men's clothing before. They were loose nearly everywhere, yet not uncomfortable. I placed my own clothes in the bag and tied that to the back of my saddle.

'Follow me,' Hugh said. He passed over the steel helmet he must have stolen on his earlier visit. 'Your hair is too obvious. Pile it under this.'

'I will look out of place wearing a helmet when I am just riding through.'

'You will look more out of place as a man with hair down to his…' Hugh changed the word quickly, 'hips.'

I smiled. Most of the men in the Lethan, including Robert, would have used a much more graphic term. 'Thank you,' I said, referring to Hugh's gentlemanly language rather than the loan of the helmet. I stacked my long hair on top of my head and fitted the helmet on top. It was heavy and uncomfortable.

'Ready?' Hugh's eyes wandered down me. 'I wish…' he said, turned his horse abruptly and walked it away.

'You wish?' I probed.

He did not finish his sentence.

Chapter Ten

LIDDESDALE
SEPTEMBER 1585

We rode down from the Nine Stane Rig where my faithfulness to Robert had been tested and my passion had emerged victorious, and we rode up Liddesdale in full view of everybody.

Now, you may not know that in the Borderland all the major people were known to each other and were recognisable by sight and by name. Despite the size of the area and the number of people, it was really quite a close community, so when we walked our horses down from the ridge and stepped boldly up the valley, I felt certain that somebody would realise we were strangers and shout out a challenge.

What I had not reckoned with was the nocturnal nature of the Borders. It was an elemental mistake I made. Hugh had not made the same error. With so many of the men engaged in night-time reiving, only women, children, and ordinary farmers were abroad in the early morning. That, added to the shifting, uncertain light of autumn and Hugh's iron nerves, worked in our favour.

I was inclined to rush, to try and pass through the valley as quickly as possible so pushed in my spurs to hurry things along.

'Slow down.' Hugh's voice was calm as his hand rested on the bridle of my horse. I could not resist the temptation to touch it. 'We are ordinary men going about our business. There is no need to rush.'

He was right of course. Respectable travellers, even in such an extraordinary locality as Liddesdale, did not rush. They move at a steady pace, as Hugh insisted we do, and nodded to people they passed, even taking the time to remark on events to whoever they met on the road.

'Well met, fellows!' The cheerful call took me by surprise, so I nearly jumped up from my saddle.

'Well met.' Hugh responded with a lift of his hand as the small group of people reined up in front of us to pass the time of day. I looked up briefly from beneath the brim of my helmet. There were five in the company, two women and three men.

'Are you bound for Hawick, friend?' The leading man seemed inclined to speak. He was a young-looking man with a neat beard and an air of obvious authority.

'Hawick and points north,' Hugh said. 'Peebles if we can get there by nightfall. And yourselves?'

The bearded man laughed. 'Hermitage Castle for a night or two,' he said, 'and maybe some sport.'

'There is ill sport in Liddesdale,' Hugh responded.

I was less interested in whatever sport this gallant young blade intended than in the attention that both women in his train were paying in me. Perhaps men believe that they can spot a pretty woman a mile away, as many of my Lethan boys claimed, but it is a fact that women are more perspicacious than men. These two were studying me and whispering together behind raised hands and with wondering, calculating eyes.

'Ill sport?' the gallant man asked. 'Why is that, pray?'

'Why, sir,' Hugh said with a laugh. 'We passed by the Castleton and Whithaugh yestreen and the whole place was astir. There were horsemen and riders galloping all around the place, beacon fires a-burning and great bands of horsemen all calling havoc and murder on the land and on the Scotts in particular.'

Now that was a blatant lie. At no time had I heard anybody crying for murder on the Scott family. The Armstrongs and the others had been intent only on the two of us. However, I saw the bearded man stiffen in his saddle at Hugh's words. 'Were they indeed?'

'That is what I heard,' my brazen liar said. 'Why, Wild Will himself was there, shouting that he would capture the Bold Buccleuch in person and hang him naked from his rooftree, him and his women and all his household.'

I said nothing, merely lowered my head from the acute examination of the two women as the bearded gallant touched a hand to the long blade he wore at his saddle. 'We'll see about that,' he said in a voice that was suddenly grim with menace. Whoever this man was, he was no earl spoiled with fur and ermines, not with that determined thrust to his jaw. Any sane man or coward would have turned back at the news that Liddesdale was riding, while this forward man signalled to a flaxen-haired youth who sat his horse two strides behind the women.

'Sound the horn,' the bearded gallant said. 'Bring our lads in closer. It seems that we shall be hunting before we reach Hermitage this day.'

As flaxen-hair lifted the horn to his lips, one of the women walked her horse to the gallant man. I held my breath as she spoke to him, nodding toward me, and then the horn sounded a long, wavering note that rose to the sky and brought a host of wild geese rising from the grassland nearby.

'We shall bid you farewell, my Lord.' Hugh touched a hand to his head.

'You know me, then?' Yet it was to me the gallant looked and not to Hugh.

'Why yes, My Lord, you are Walter Scott of Buccleuch.' Hugh touched spurs to his horse and walked on, with me a hands-breadth behind him with my heart in my mouth. The gallant was Walter

Scott of Buccleuch himself: The Bold Buccleuch, the man who led the mighty Scott family, able to call up three thousand Border lances at a lift of his little pinkie. And as I watched I realised why Hugh had made up his tales about the Armstrongs. All along the ridges on both sides of us, men appeared, carrying their lances in their right hands.

'Ride on,' I said, 'quickly.'

'Safe journey to you, friend.' Scott of Buccleuch lifted a hand to Hugh. 'And to you, my lady.' His smile to me was entirely conspiratorial. Suddenly my disguise did not seem impenetrable in the slightest and my thoughts that men were not as perceptive as women also seemed wide of the mark. I mustered a half-hearted smile, kicked in my spurs, and rode on, feeling very vulnerable and just a little humiliated.

'We need no longer worry about the Armstrongs,' Hugh said. 'With Scott of Buccleuch and his men riding through Liddesdale they will have enough to contend with.'

I nodded. Until that moment I had been more concerned with discovery than anything else but now more personal matters came once more to the fore. I thought of what I had done and how it altered my entire perception of myself. I had allowed my baser instincts to take over. I had betrayed Robert. I had failed myself and my family.

How could I face him? We had been friends all my life. We had made an agreement to wed and we had been faithful to each other until I gave way to my own weakness and my own passion. How could I tell him? What could I say?

'You are quiet,' Hugh said as we negotiated a pass between long green hills. I heard the call of a yorling and remembered that laughing, enigmatic man who had begun this whole adventure. Whoever he was, he had started a long train that led to my downfall and personal discovery.

'I am thinking.' I looked sideways at him.

'About what we did last night?' Hugh asked.

'About what we did last night.' I said no more.

'I will come with you if you decide to tell Robert,' Hugh said. 'If he decides to kill me then the world will be rid of an ugly man. I will die knowing that my world could never get any better than it was with you.'

I did not say that my world would also have been the poorer if I had not experienced the previous night. I was learning. Instead, I nodded. 'It is kind of you to say that.'

'It is no kindness,' he snapped that, which pleased me although I could not say why.

'I do not wish you to be there if I tell Robert. You are at feud with us; my Tweedies would kill you as soon as you appeared near the Lethan.' That was only the truth. It was another reason that I was confused, for if I admitted that I had bedded a Veitch I would be even less thought of.

'You do not have to tell him,' Hugh said. 'That would be the simplest solution. Or perhaps...'

'Or perhaps?' I hoped for a solution to my problem.

'You do not have to return to the Lethan,' Hugh spoke quietly. He reached across and took hold of Kailzie's bridle. 'There are other valleys just as sweet, other towers as comfortable as Cardrona and other men who want you as much as Robert Ferguson does.'

I shook my head. 'I have given my word,' I said. 'And there is more.'

'What more is there?'

We reined up there, with that evil valley of Liddesdale behind us and ahead, the ragged road leading us home to Peebles-shire and the Lethan Valley. The sun had risen, casting our elongated shadows long and dark over the autumnal heather until they merged together at the head. I faced Hugh and told him what nobody else knew except my mother.

He listened in silence until I had finished. 'You saw yourself with Robert in a vision?' he asked.

'Every year on my birthday.' I waited for the inevitable ridicule. People who have not experienced such things tend to mock, either through fear or scepticism, which is one reason that I did not tell anybody. My other reason was through fear of being called a witch.

Hugh neither mocked nor called me a follower of Satan. 'I have never met anybody with such a power before.' If anything, he sounded sad rather than doubtful. Releasing the bridle of my horse, he began to move again. 'When I heard your voice in the dungeon, I knew that you were above the common set of people, and as soon as I saw your face, I knew you were a most noble piece of work, a paragon.'

'I am none of that,' I told him. I did not tell him of the ache in my heart every time I looked at him, or the lust in my loins. Some things are better left unsaid when one is riding alone with a vibrant man in the stark hills of the Borderland. Nor did I tell him of my sense of desolation when I compared him to my Robert. That, I decided, must remain forever unsaid and only admitted to myself.

'You have given your word.' Hugh seemed to have accepted my visions without a qualm. 'It is a sign of a wonderful woman to keep your word after so long.'

My hurt made me turn on him with some heat. 'Is it a sign of a wonderful woman to bed a strange man within the Nine Stane Rig?'

His silence was eloquent of the pain my words caused him. I know that men have the ability to hurt women with their physical strength. I did not then know that the best of men are vulnerable to equally deep hurt by the words of women for whom they care. We are a careless sex with our tongues, injuring sometimes without consideration and driving pain deep within the hearts of those we love and who love us most. Sometime a wise king may pass a law protecting women from the hands of men. It will need to be a wiser queen to pass a similar law protecting men from the tongues of women.

I do not know how long our silence endured but we were many miles from Liddesdale before Hugh spoke again. He continued our conversation as if there had been no gap.

'Am I still that strange a man? I find it unlikely that a woman such as you would bed a man she thinks a stranger.'

I had also been thinking. 'A woman such as myself has a hot desire,' I said, still tart, 'and perhaps that desire will overcome any objections to the strangeness of the man I happen to be with.' Although the words were mainly directed toward myself, Hugh visibly flinched. I had hurt him again. I learned again how easy it is to hurt a man who loves you. It is the ones you hurt that matter most, always. If they did not care, they would not feel the wounds our tongues create. We do damage to our loves by such behaviour and wonder why our men seek solace with others with gentler words and comforting bodies. A woman's tongue is too potent a weapon to be misused.

'So, I was just one among many then.' Hugh had been stung to retaliate and I did not like his response. 'A woman of your ardent desire must have bedded many men, strange or not, in her lifetime.' It may have been chance that he rode an arms-length away rather than with our knees near touching but I rather fancied that he was pulling away physically as I lambasted him verbally.

Hurt by his words, I responded by inflicting more pain, hating myself while searching for venom. 'You are just one,' I told him. 'A man I met while on a journey, a male body on which to slake my lust. Nothing more.'

I could not have wounded him deeper or said words that were further from the truth. He turned away from me, a man who had sought grace from a graceless face and found vindictiveness when he hoped for a spirit as generous as his own. I should have apologised then; I should have withdrawn my barbed words and thrown myself on my knees to beg mercy from the kindest and most noble man I had ever met. Instead, I tore the helmet from my head and threw it into the rough heather at the side of the road, allowed my hair to flow freely down my back and kicked in my spurs so I cantered ahead of him. Let him see my back, I thought, and the set of my shoulders. Insufferable man!

We rode like that, with me forging the path northward to Tweeddale and Hugh two horse-lengths behind. I nursed my wrath, keeping it warm as I told myself that Hugh had wronged me with his words and he deserved my scorn and vituperation, while all the time feeling the desolation of loss fighting the anger I stoked. Behind me, I did not know how Hugh felt. Sometimes I wished that he would spur forward, tip me off my horse and drag me into the heather to treat me as he had done so well within the Nine Stone Rig. I did not know, then, that good men did not act so. Good men gave their women respect and love; they did not act in such an ungentlemanly manner. I wished for Hugh to turn into a brute beast while still retaining his essential kindly qualities. Such things do not happen: Hugh was a gentleman in all the best meanings of the word. He remained behind me, silent, perhaps brooding, and despite my gnawing temper and the lingering sting of my words, I knew that he would look after me if a mishap occurred on the road. There was a word for that; a word that I dared not say although within me I knew what it was.

That word was love. Hugh had voiced it and I had rejected it, yet my rejection had not nullified the reality, only pushed it aside. I knew that Hugh loved me; men like him did not say such things without consideration and thought. I also knew that I loved him.

That was a love that could never be admitted if I wished peace of mind. It was a word that turned itself over within my mind and tore great holes in my heart. It was a forbidden love that had caused me to react with such venom. I hated that love for destroying the certainty of my life and because I rejected that love I also rejected the cause and fountain of it. I hated Hugh for making me love him. In that confused oxymoron of emotions, I rode along that damp track through the stark green hills of the Borders with my mood becoming fouler by the mile.

When I was not hoping for Hugh to come to me, I wished only to be left alone with my thoughts, my unfair anger, and my sense of impending loss. As I alternated between hatred and love, I did not want to see Hugh leave me, and leave me he must for with the feud between our surnames, he would be in grave danger the instant he rode into the Lethan Valley.

'Horsemen ahead.' They were the first words that Hugh had spoken for hours. They jerked me out of my reverie and into the reality of our physical situation. I looked around and recognised where we were. The surrounding hills were only a dozen miles from the Lethan, with familiar shapes and friendly outlines. There was a late-season laverock trilling above, perhaps even that same bird I had heard as we harvested the crops only a few days and a lifetime ago. I could not see any horsemen.

'A round score,' Hugh continued, 'moving slowly.'

I wondered whether I wished to talk to him yet. 'Where?' I could spare a single word. It did not mean that I liked him, only that I had decided it was necessary to recognise his existence: nothing more.

'They are in front and on the hills on either side.' Hugh was more loquacious. 'Four are on the road and the others are supporting. I can hear the rattle of equipment, so they are armed.'

'All men are armed on the road!' I injected a sneer into my words, still aiming to hurt him and feeling the stab of pain in my own heart.

I heard Hugh unsheathe his sword. 'Keep close, My Lady Jeannie,' he said quietly. 'They may not be our friends.'

I nearly turned to face him. Instead, I reined in just slightly, just enough to obey his advice but not enough, certainly not enough, to allow him to think that he mattered to me.

The horsemen appeared on the crest of the hill to my right, and then to my left. They rode in line abreast, each man with his lance and sword, each one with the steel helmet firm on his head, each one with the high morning sun on his face. Eight on each side and four on the road, exactly as Hugh had said, and I knew each man by name and reputation, by family and history.

'Father!' I nearly screamed the word as I saw Father at the head, with his homely bearded face set, and then, 'Robert!' For Robert rode at his side, sturdy, freckled Robert Ferguson, my own, my very own Robert riding south to rescue me.

Without a thought I shouted his name and put spurs to my horse, waving my hand in delight. And so, I bade farewell to Hugh Veitch and rode to Robert. And my destiny. I hardly looked back, thinking that Hugh would be behind me.

'Father!' I galloped to him as he spurred to meet me, shouting my name. The others, the vanguard of the armed might of the Tweedies of the Lethan Valley rode down from the hills to see me. We met in a maelstrom of shouts and a confusion of embraces and laughter, with Robert all a-grin and the boys of the Lethan asking a hundred questions.

'Where did you get that horse from?' Robert asked. 'She's a beauty.'

It was such a typical Robert response that I had to laugh and my father embraced me in his great bear-like arms as his grizzled beard tickled my face and his nose pressed against mine.

'You are well?'

'I am well,' I said excitedly, smiling into his wise, worried old eyes.

'We were coming for you.' Father indicated the men who rode at his side.

'We were going to rescue you!' Robert seemed excited at the prospect. 'We found out that you were down in Liddesdale.'

'I was there,' I said. 'Wild Will Armstrong held us prisoner. Hugh and I escaped...' I looked around for Hugh. The excitement at meeting Father and Robert had quite driven my anger away and I was prepared to forgive him. I expected him to fall in with my moods, you see; I was a very thoughtless young woman in these days. 'Where is Hugh?'

'Hugh?' Father raised grizzled eyebrows. 'Who is Hugh?' The sun caught the ring on his pinkie as he reached for his sword.

'He is the man I escaped with.' I looked around, expecting to see his face among the familiar men of the Lethan. He was not there so I cast my gaze further back lest he was lurking at the fringes, waiting to be invited. That was the sort of thing a gentleman would do, I reckoned. 'I cannot see him.'

'You were alone,' Robert said. 'There was no man with you. You were alone on the road when we saw you.'

'No.' I shook my head so vehemently that my hair netted across my face and I had to claw it free. 'I was with Hugh. You must have seen him.'

'There was nobody with you,' Father said.

I eased out of the press and looked back; the road was as empty as the hills. There was no sign of Hugh anywhere. I had a sudden feeling of dread as if I was wrong and Hugh had been somebody I dreamed up, or perhaps, horribly the spirit of the Tweed. We had made love once, when my Robert had been absent and we were in an ancient, sacred place, filled with the power of those stones.

No. I shook those silly thoughts away. Hugh had been real; he had been as solid and real as any of the men in whose company I now stood. I had not imagined him or dredged him from some recess of my imagination. Or, God forbid, he had not emerged from the haunted Tweed to enchant me with his love and leave me with a spirit-child.

Oh, dear God in heaven! That was a possibility that I was with child!

I tried to calm my fears as I forced a smile. 'He must have gone another way,' I said. 'It is not important.'

'Who was this Hugh?' Robert asked. As always, he was like the cow's tail, always at the back. Even so, it was good to see his face.

'He was just a man I escaped with and who travelled the road with me.' I tried to sound as casual as possible. 'As I said, he was not important.' I dismissed Hugh and his love with as little apparent concern as if he had been a mouse I had passed or a bird of the sky.

'We will get you back home,' Father decided, 'and we will hear of your adventures.' He stepped back, holding my shoulders in both hands. 'You are looking well for somebody who was held by the Armstrongs.'

'I was not held long,' I said, still searching hopefully for Hugh. 'They only had me for a day or so after the Yorling grabbed me.'

I saw my father's face alter and knew there was something he was not telling me. This was not the time to ask. I wanted to go home. I also wanted Hugh. I knew I could not have both.

Father looked me up and down, shaking his head. 'Did they force you to wear men's clothing?'

I had forgotten that I was dressed like a man. 'No,' I said. 'We put these on so we could ride through Liddesdale in safety.'

'Tell me when we get home,' Father said again, as Robert asked me about Kailzie.

Chapter Eleven

LETHAN VALLEY
OCTOBER 1585

Can you remember the parable about the prodigal son and how his father killed the fatted calf when he returned home? Well, that did not happen at my homecoming. Instead, Mother looked me up and down, said: 'aye; you're home then,' and got on with her spinning. That was my welcome back to Cardrona Tower. No fanfares, no beating of drums, or sounding of trumpets. A few words and a look, yet I was still glad to be home, in familiar surroundings and surrounded by friendly faces.

Yet although everything was the same, everything seemed different. It was not of course: the Lethan was the same; it was me that had changed. I had been outside the confines of the Lethan Valley, I had experienced violence and theft, I had met a great many very unpleasant men and I had my first visitation of the Tweedie Passion. In short, I was a woman now while before I had been a girl.

However, other things had also changed in my enforced absence, as I discovered the morning after my return. I lay in my own bed, staring at the groined ceiling, thinking how glad I was to be back home and wondering about Hugh when Mother walked in.

Expecting her to start shouting that I should be up and about and working, I sat up and swung my legs over the edge of the bed.

'Don't get up.' Mother held up her hand to stop me. She sat on the bed at my side. 'Now that you've decided to come back,' Mother spoke as if I had chosen to be abducted and carried away by half the outlaws of the Borders, 'your Father will want to talk to you.'

I nodded. 'I have already told him what happened.' Or some of it, anyway. I missed out some minor details, such as what Hugh and I had got up to, and the fact that he had been a Veitch.

'So I believe,' Mother said. 'It is what you have not said that I find most interesting. We will discuss that later.' She looked deep into my eyes. 'You have much to tell me, I believe.'

I said nothing to that.

'If I were you,' Mother said. 'I would get up and dressed soon. And get a decent breakfast. You will need all the strength today.'

I shoved back the tangled mess of my hair and scratched my head. Honestly, if men saw us first thing in the morning, they would not be attracted at all. Mind you, Hugh had first seen me in a dungeon, filthy and… I concentrated on what Mother had said. 'Why?' I asked. I had rather hoped that I could recover after all my recent excitements.

'You'll see.' Mother patted my thigh. 'It's up to your father to explain, not me.' She lowered her voice. 'All I will say is don't think too hardly of him, Jeannie. Talk to me later, when you know.'

'When I know what?' I scratched my head again, furiously, and again pushed back my shocking hair. I hated all this secrecy. Why could people not be straightforward and open? 'Why should I think hardly of Father?'

Mother patted my thigh again. 'We are having a visitor in the forenoon,' she said. 'Some things will be explained then.' She looked at me, sighed, and shook her head. 'I will send up a maid with a basin of water to help wash your hair, Jeannie. I can see you brought half of Liddesdale back with you. If I did not know better, I would say that you had been rolling around on the ground.'

You will have to do better than that, Mother, I thought. 'It would feel cleaner after a wash.'

'And wear something at last half-decent,' Mother said, 'don't go around near naked.' She stood up, shaking her head. 'It's no wonder most of the men in the Borders want to bed you.'

I was better than half-decent when I sat at the ingleneuk in the great hall. I had taken pains with both my clothes and my appearance, which drew some ribald comments from the boys of the valley when they began to filter in. The maid had done herself proud in washing my hair with water in which birch-bark had been soaked so it both shone and had a sweet aroma. That caused Robert to give a loud laugh.

'Is that the latest fashion in Liddesdale?'

I did not fully appreciate the joke and told him so with hot words and narrowed eyes that did their work well.

'It was meant to be funny,' Robert said.

About to say that it would have been funnier if he had come to rescue me, I bit back the words. I had no desire to humiliate him further. Indeed, I knew he was going to save me at some time in the future, so I had to be gentle with him. I swallowed my anger.

'Do you know what this is all about?' I asked.

'Not yet,' Robert said, smiling past me to Crooked Sim of the Mains.

'Does anybody know?' I looked around the hall as more men entered. All the leading men of the valley seemed to be there, from our tenants at Lethanhead away up in the hills to the riverside men of Lethanfoot who owed their allegiance to Ferguson of Whitecleuch.

'What?' Robert glanced at me. 'Oh, no I don't think so, Jeannie. Not until your father tells us.'

'It's good to be back.' I reached out for him.

When Robert continued to ignore me and talk to Crooked Sim, I nudged him in the ribs. 'I said it's good to be back!' I nodded to my hand. Honestly, that man was hard work. 'You may take my hand if you wish.'

'Go on, Rab, take her hand when you're told,' Crooked Sim jeered. 'Jeannie got herself all dressed up for you! She even washed the lice from her hair.'

I tapped my hand on the table we sat around. 'Robert?'

He laughed and looked away. 'Not in front of my friends, Jeannie,' he said so softly that only I could hear him.

I withdrew my hand and stood up. 'I will leave you with your friends,' I said.

There was a better view from the top table and anyway, it was where I belonged. I should never have joined the Whitecleuch boys, despite Robert being there. I sat at the top table with a vacant seat on either side, fuming as more men crammed into the hall and my Robert sat in the midst of his cronies, cracking poor jokes, and boasting to each other of their prowess.

Only after the last of my father's chief tenants found a space did Father himself arrive, with Mother at his side. Father entered with a flourish and with his sword at his side, which was unusual inside the tower.

As the men either stood in respect or hammered hard hands on the table in spontaneous applause, Father and Mother stepped to the head table, with Willie Telfer standing by the closed door. I moved aside as they took their places.

'Enough!' Father roared and the row gradually subsided. 'You will be wondering why I have gathered you all together today.' That was a statement rather than a question. 'Well if you sit still and listen you will learn.'

There was a general laugh at that, with a few ribald comments from the more crude of the men. Why do some men think it amusing to be rude about everything?

'For as long as we all can remember,' Father said, 'we have been at feud with the Veitches.'

The men growled at that, waving their fists in the air to prove their martial valour and dislike of the old enemy. I sat silent, thinking of Hugh as I watched Robert and his group of friends outshout all the others; young callants eager to be heard. For one bitter moment I wondered how they would fare against Wild Will and his band of veteran outlaws, shook the thought away as disloyal and listened to Father.

'We have bickered for decades. They have raided us, and we have raided them; we have reived a few cattle and they have reived a few cattle; we have burned a couple of their cottages and they have burned a couple of our cottages. There have been some killings.'

Father paused then to allow the men of the Lethan remember the men and women they had lost to the vicious Veitches and savour the triumph of victory as the brave Tweedies had exacted revenge by catching and killing a handful of the enemy over the decades.

'It is time to end this once and for all,' Father declared.

I was the only person who clapped in the ensuing hush. The feud with the Veitches had been a fact for so long that people could not think of an alternative. Now I believed that Father was proposing an end to the feud, so we could live in peace.

Father raised his hands high. 'It is time that we finally quelled the Veitches and turned their lands into a smoking waste; put their men to the sword, burned their crops, reived their livestock, and razed their towers to the ground!'

I stopped clapping, appalled that Father intended the very opposite of what I had hoped. 'No!' I said. Now my small voice was lost in the roar of approval from the assembled might of the Lethan Valley. The Tweedies and their tenants were on their feet shouting their delight at the thought of turning a smouldering feud into a full-scale war.

'Father!' I shouted, 'you can't!' I remembered Liddesdale where men carried weapons every day, where the churches and chapels had been destroyed, where the only law was the blade and the hangman's rope. I did not wish my green Lethan Valley turned into a place like that.

'You hear my daughter!' Father calmed his people down. 'She has immediately realised the reason we have not done this before is that we lacked the numbers.'

'No, Father,' I protested, 'that is not what I meant.' About to explain, I found Mother's hands on me as she ushered me back to my seat.

'Hush Jeannie; this is Father's day. He has a lot to explain.' Mother's eyes were deep with warning.

I sat down and clamped shut my mouth. I knew I spoke too much. I also knew that I did not wish to see Father, brave though he was, pitted against active, proven fighters such as Hugh Veitch. I certainly did not wish to see Robert outmatched again.

'We have not done this before,' Father continued, 'because we have lacked the manpower. We have two hundred riders in the Lethan; the Veitches have three hundred. If we faced them in open battle, they would outnumber us.'

The assembly was silent again. They knew these facts, of course, but hearing them was always sobering.

'I was as aware of the numbers as you are,' Father spoke more quietly now, 'so I cast a wide net to look for allies and distant kinsmen.'

That got my interest. The old Border worked on the kin system. Family was second only to business. Men and women felt strong attachment to family, and blood and loyalty could be fierce unless cattle were involved. I had thought the Tweedies were a close-knit family; I was not aware that we had kin outside the Lethan Valley.

'Let me introduce you to one of them.' Father nodded to Willie Telfer at the door. 'Right, Willie; bring him in.'

When Willie opened the door and a man stepped in, a buzz ran around the great hall. I watched in astonishment as the Yorling, resplendent in his bright yellow jack and with his spurs rattling, stepped across the stone flags.

I stood up, reaching for some sort of weapon, as a score of men did the same. I searched for Robert's gaze, hoping to reassure him that I believed in him despite his discomfiture at the hands of this lithe young man.

There was a smile on the face of the Yorling as he joined us at the top table. He gave a small bow to Mother, and a deeper bow to me.

'I am glad to see you alive and well, My Lady Jean,' he said quietly as the assembly broke into a hundred questions.

I responded with stiff formality. 'Sir,' I said, with the briefest of curtseys.

Father banged his fist on the table for silence, causing great dents in the pine for which Mother would undoubtedly later take him to task.

'Most of you have heard of the Yorling.' Father had to raise his voice and repeat himself until the hubbub died down. 'Well; I have a small admission to make.'

As the Yorling stood beside Father, I drew in my breath sharply. I had always been aware that I felt a bond to the Yorling; despite his actions, I had known that I was never in any real danger from him. Now I guessed why.

I looked toward Mother and felt her hand slide around mine. 'Mother...' I said.

'Yes, Jeannie,' she whispered. 'I already know.'

I squeezed my mother's hand in sympathy and support.

'Some of you may have guessed the truth,' Father said. 'In my youth, before I met my lady wife, I was a roving blade.'

Most of the men laughed at that, digging each other in the ribs and guffawing their masculine approval. Oh, our Tweedie men loved to think of themselves as men's men, reiving and raiding for women as well as cattle, although in slightly different ways. I hoped.

'In these old days, I roved around the Debateable Land and had a name and reputation. I wore a yellow jack most remarkably like this one and men knew me as the Yorling.'

That name caused a hush to fall on the gathering. Everybody had heard of the Yorling as the leader of an outlaw band decades before. Now they knew that my Father, Tweedie of the Lethan, had been that man. I am sure their opinion of him multiplied. I am not sure that I shared their adulation.

'This bold young callant took on my mantle.' Father tapped the Yorling's shoulder. 'This is George, now known as George Graham from his mother's side, or the Yorling. He is my son; born out of wedlock so not able to inherit my lands, but Tweedie by blood.'

I had guessed that truth and now I looked on the face of the half-brother I had not known that I possessed. He looked at me along the length of the table.

'Will you forgive me, my sister?' His smile was as wide as ever although there was genuine concern in his smokey eyes. 'You were never in danger.'

'I always knew that,' I said truthfully, 'but why did you do it?'

As he opened his mouth to talk, Father started again. 'Now you see why the time is right to rid us of the plague of the Veitches. George—the Yorling—will add his band of twenty riders to our strength and our combined force will sweep the Veitches from their land of Faladale!'

The gathering were on their feet, clapping hands and stamping feet, hammering the tables with fists, tankards, and the pommels of daggers as they agreed full-heartedly with Father's ideas.

Oh, Father was clever. He had used his youthful faults as a tool to give the valley exactly what they wanted. Now nobody could accuse him of anything except being a vibrant youth, a man with the Tweedie Passion, which all knew about and nobody would gainsay.

'Mother…' I leaned closer to her, embarrassed that her husband's philandering should be so publicly revealed.

Mother shook her head. 'We are all Tweedies now,' she said softly and stood up.

'I wish to speak!' Mother said, and silence fell on the gathering as men and the few women waited to hear what the Lady Lethan had to say about her husband's bastard son.

'George!' Mother said loudly. 'Welcome to our surname, our valley, and our family!'

She sat down again as the great hall erupted in a huge roar of approval and probably relief. All knew that my mother was a formidable woman, well able to take care of herself verbally and physically. Now they had heard her formally accept the issue of Father's pre-marital loins into her household there was no reason for any other to take issue. George Graham, the Yorling, was accepted as part of the Tweedies of Lethan Valley.

'Now the Veitches will pay the reckoning in full, and we shall sign the deeds of their repentance in red ink and with a sharp quill!' Father said as the gathering roared approval of bloodshed, violence, and death. I slipped away with my head confused and my eyes stinging with hot tears. I was not sure why.

Chapter Twelve

LETHAN VALLEY
OCTOBER 1585

'So, I have a brother.' I did not soften my words with a preamble.

Father looked up from the table where he was eating, with half a leg of reived mutton before him and a flagon of good claret. 'You have a brother,' he confirmed. I could tell by the narrowing of his eyes that he expected me to lay blame on him. I could not do that after my experience with Hugh.

'I always wanted a brother,' I said and saw Father's expression soften.

'We all need kin,' he said.

I nodded at that. 'I think there is more you need to tell me, Father.' I slid onto a bench opposite him, folding my skirt neatly beneath me. 'Such as why he rode into the valley and abducted me.'

Father could never look innocent. His attempt was ludicrous, with spreading hands and wide-open eyes. 'Why should I know that?'

'Because you know everything that happens in this valley.' I held his gaze. 'And you knew he was your son.' I tapped my fingers on the table, copying Mother's gestures when she insisted on a reply. 'You knew he was coming, Father, and you allowed him to ride free. I noticed that there were no injuries in the fighting and only one young lad was taken captive.'

Father's smile was wide and as reassuring as a cat's gape at a mouse hole. 'Yes, Jeannie, I arranged the Yorling's attack.'

'Why?' I said. 'And none of your lies, Father. I am in no mood to brook more falsehoods.'

'Oh?' Father raised his eyebrows. 'The fox cub threatens the old wolf.' His laugh was loud and equally perfidious. 'I arranged that raid to capture you, of course, my daughter. Oh, you were never in any danger. George would not have hurt a hair on your cossetted little head.'

'So why then?' I asked.

'Why do you think?' Father asked. 'You have an understanding with Robert of Whitecleuch. The two of you have promised all sorts of foolish things ever since childhood.'

I had thought that Father did not care one way or another whether I married Robert. Now I looked into his devious face and realised that he had been watching everything all the time and hatching his own plans for my future. 'Carry on, Father,' I said.

'Robert of Whitecleuch will not be a good leader for Tweedies,' Father said seriously. 'He is slow, ponderous, and cannot wield a sword. When I asked the Yorling to take you away, I had one of two things in mind.'

I am not sure how I felt when I heard that Father had arranged that I should be abducted by a group of men I had never met in my life. 'What were these two things, Father?'

'Either Robert would finally prove himself a man,' Father said, 'Or he would make such a fool of himself that you would finally see how useless he was for you and the valley, and you would choose somebody more suitable.'

'So, the entire raid was false?' I said.

'It was all false,' Father said.

'Robert did not know that,' I said. 'He might have killed the Yorling, my brother George.'

Father's great laugh boomed out around his chamber. 'Robert could not hurt the Yorling if he tried for a month!' The idea seemed to amuse him so much that I felt my anger build up.

'Robert's not that bad,' I said. 'At least he came to look for me.'

Father's laughter ended abruptly. 'If your mother had been taken by a raiding party, I would be in the saddle and raising a hot trod within half an hour. Robert did not do that.'

I said nothing. I remembered how tenderly the Yorling had treated me in his ride away from the Lethan Valley, and how he had camped high on the hill with few precautions. At the time I had thought it bold; now I saw that he was not hiding from Robert but allowing him the opportunity to track and capture me back, if he so willed.

'The Yorling tells me that while he awaited Robert's trod, Wild Will came instead,' Father said.

'That is how it happened,' I agreed. I remembered that professional onslaught by the Armstrongs and the ease with which they had overcome the Yorling's men. I had not realised, then, that the Yorling had been inviting such an attack and so their resistance had been slight.

'The Yorling lost one man killed and another badly hurt in that encounter,' Father said, 'and spent the next two days tracking Wild Will to Tarras. He knew he could not defeat the Armstrongs in their own stronghold so came back for me and the men of Lethan.'

I nodded. 'My Robert was with you,' I reminded.

'He was,' Father said. 'He came to me for help when he should have been on the trail of the Yorling and then on that of Wild Will.'

Despite myself, I shuddered at the thought of my Robert tracking the Armstrongs through Liddesdale and the desolation of the Tarras Moss.

'At least he came looking for me.' I defended him.

Father raised his eyebrows and said nothing to that.

'Are you still intent on marrying him?' Father asked.

'I am,' I said stoutly. Father knew about my visions. I had no need to remind him.

'I thought so,' Father said. 'That is the main reason I want to remove any threat from the Veitches. With Robert Ferguson as the head of the surname, the Tweedies will be every man's prey.' He lifted the tankard of ale that stood beside his right hand. 'In other words, Jeannie, although you do not approve of what I am doing, I am ensuring your safety, and that of my people.' He took a deep draught of the ale and put the tankard down with a thump. 'Mostly yours.'

I knew I should thank him. Instead, I could only say, 'There could be a lot of people killed.'

'They will only be Veitch corpses if the men do as they are told,' Father said, 'and if your fool Robert does not fall off his horse or cut his finger on his sword or allow a ten-year-old child to unhorse him.'

It hurt to hear Father's low opinion of Robert. It hurt more when I knew he was only slightly exaggerating. I knew that Robert had so many good points, yet I could never convince others to see them. One day though Robert would ride over a ridge and save me; he would prove himself as bold a hero as any man in the Borders.

'I am not inclined to let this thing wait,' Father said. 'Word will reach the Veitches that the Yorling and his men have arrived in the valley. They will guess that we are going to attack them and will prepare, so we must strike soon.'

I thought of Hugh and knew I did not want him hurt. 'How soon, Father?'

'In a day or so,' Father said.

I felt fear for Hugh, and fear for Robert facing the Veitches. If they were all of Hugh's standard then Robert, and Father, would be facing a redoubtable foe.

'Now,' Father said, 'I have things to work out and arrangements to make. If you have nothing to do, then I am sure your mother can find something for you.'

'I am sure she would,' I said, 'and that sounds a very good reason to avoid her company.'

Father's smile was genuine this time. 'Go and find your man,' he said. 'Maybe you can get some sense into him. God knows that nobody else has been able to. I have something to tidy up.'

Robert was in the stables, helping a groom rub down his horse. As was common in the Lethan Valley, the men rode stallions or geldings and left the mares for women.

'You can go now.' I dismissed the groom. 'We won't be needing you for the next hour or so.'

Handing his curry comb to Robert, the groom left at once.

'They are nearly as scared of you as they are of your mother,' Robert said.

'I am not scary,' I said.

'You can be.' Robert knelt down to inspect the legs of his horse. He glanced at me over his shoulder. 'The servants are scared of you.'

I knelt at his side. 'Are you?'

'I'm not scared of anything!' There was that boastful Robert again, so false and so different from the caring Robert looking after his horse. I much preferred his caring side.

I put a hand on his shoulder. 'Thank you for coming to search for me,' I said.

He shied away from my touch before relaxing. 'I'm glad you are unhurt,' he said. 'You said that you escaped with a man. Who was he?'

'Just another prisoner of the Armstrongs.' I dismissed Hugh with a casual shrug. 'We got out together. Why did you not want to talk to me in the great hall?'

Robert looked back at his horse. 'I was with the lads,' he said. 'I did not want to look soft by talking to a girl. They laugh at me.'

I took a deep breath, fighting my temper. That was the sort of reply I would have expected when he was twelve years old. 'That was an honest answer,' I said. 'I'll remember not to approach you when you are with them.'

I resolved to talk to his friends one by one. If the servants thought I was scary then so help me I would put the fear of God into these little boys who sought to keep Robert and me apart by mocking him. That was for the future.

'Robert.' I inched closer so my thigh touched his. He continued to examine the horse. 'Robert!'

He looked around.

'Can you leave that blasted horse for a moment and talk to me?'

Robert looked comically surprised. 'I am talking to you, Jeannie. Do you think this tendon is a trifle weak? I have to ride him soon and I don't want to damage him.'

'No, you don't want a lame horse,' I agreed. 'I will leave you two alone together.'

I walked away and sent the groom back in. Once again, I felt like crying. I had known Robert all my life, my visions told me that he would be my man, and yet I seemed unable to communicate with him. We remained friends and nothing else. I felt as if I was running out of time.

Chapter Thirteen

LETHAN VALLEY
OCTOBER 1585

My mother, of course, noticed the difference in me since I returned from Tarras Moss. She allowed me a week to think things over, a week in which we lost three cattle to a Veitch raid and the Yorling got to know the men of the valley. A young servant gave me the message that Mother wished to see me.

'Her Ladyship was insistent,' the girl said.

'She always is,' I told her, sighed, and made my way to my mother's chamber.

Mother sat by her spinning wheel. She looked deep into my eyes. 'You are a woman now,' she said.

About to deny it, I knew that would be pointless. 'I am,' I said.

'So now you know.' Mother bent her head to her spinning. 'Was it the Tweedie Passion?'

'It was all of that,' I said. I expected her to ask who I had bedded, but she did not.

'You will be more ready to bed Robert Ferguson then,' Mother said, without looking up. She worked the foot pedal, so the spinning wheel hummed rhythmically.

'I may not be able to do that,' I said quietly. 'Or not unless he is a very forgiving man.'

Mother looked up with a strange, crooked smile on her face. 'Oh? And why is that, pray?'

'I am no longer whole,' I said. 'As we just discussed. I am no longer virginal.'

The expression on Mother's face did not alter. 'Do you think that Robert has never known a woman? He is twenty-one and the heir of Whitecleuch.'

'Robert would never betray me in that way,' I began hotly until I realised what mother had said. 'He is the younger son; he is not heir. That is one of the reasons that you do not think him a fit husband for me.'

'No Ferguson of Whitecleuch is a fit husband for a Tweedie of Lethan,' Mother said, 'be he heir or be he bastard; you are of superior blood and bearing. That is a fact. However, the situation changed last night. Robert's brother had a bit of an accident.'

'What happened?' I asked.

'He died,' Mother said flatly. He was up at the summer shieling bringing in the cattle and he did not come home. The Fergusons found his body this morning at the foot of Posso Craig; it looks as if he lost his footing at night and fell over the craigs. Dead as a three-day old corpse, which means that Robert is now heir.'

I knew Posso Craigs well, a semi-circular hill with one end sheered away in vicious cliffs. It was an accident inviting a victim.

'Now that Robert is heir to Whitecleuch,' Mother said, without expressing any regret for the passing of his unfortunate brother, 'the situation here, as I said, has altered. Even as heir to the lands, Robert is a poor choice for a husband. However, given that his lands abut ours and are at the bottom of the valley, it would be advantageous if you and Robert were wed.'

I stared at her. This was my Mother, cold-bloodedly telling me that although Robert was not a suitable man, she would favour our marriage to blend our lands together. Of course, as the senior house, Robert would become Robert of Lethan; he may even take the name of Tweedie, in fact, I would insist on that, but we all knew who the real power would be.

Mother would be in control of the entire Lethan Valley from the headwaters at Lethanhead to Lethanfoot where the Lethan Water drained into the mighty Tweed, and from where the Spirit of the Tweed had emerged to woo my distant ancestor. That was a story I no longer found unbelievable.

'I remember you telling me that he would not be a suitable husband until he proved himself as a man,' I said, with more heat than I intended.

'Situations change, Jeannie.' When Mother glanced up from her spinning her eyes were every bit as hard as Wild Will's had been. 'You had no interest in Robert's older brother. He was going to marry the daughter of a burgess in Peebles, a man who did not belong to any significant family; a nobody. We would have controlled him without any effort. Now that Robert is heir to the land, anything could happen.'

I sat down on a creepie stool, the three-legged stools that we used where we did not have chairs. 'I have long known I would marry Robert; if he will still have me.'

Mother sighed and looked up from her spinning. 'You bedded a man,' she said. 'You are a Tweedie woman. The wonder is that you waited so long.'

'There was nobody I desired so much,' I said.

She faced me. 'Now you have tasted that desire, you will never lose it. It will come on you when you least expect it and you will have to slake it.'

As I thought of Hugh, the desire that Mother spoke of increased. I felt my heartbeat increase and the strangest prickling sensation in a very personal place. 'Yes, Mother.'

'That may not always be with Robert,' Mother said calmly. 'A husband is for duty; pleasure you may have to seek otherwise.'

I felt my mouth open in astonishment. My mother was advising me to commit adultery.

'It is the Tweedie way,' Mother said without any expression on her face.

'Did you…?' I could not complete the question.

'I am not a Tweedie by blood,' Mother said.

'Father?'

'He is all Tweedie,' Mother said flatly.

'Oh.' For the first time in my life, I reached out to offer support to my mother. I squeezed her arm. 'I did not realise.'

'Well, now you do,' Mother said. 'There are many little Tweedie bastards running about the Borders. You have met at least one of them.'

For one terrible, horrible moment I thought of Hugh until I remembered that he had been a Veitch. However lusty he may be, Father would not have bedded one of our enemies. 'The Yorling,' I said.

'The Yorling,' Mother said. 'There are others. More importantly, I want you to make sure you wed Robert.'

'He will know I am not whole…' I gestured down at myself as I blurted out the stark physical fact.

Mother snorted. 'For God's sake woman! Is that all that's bothering you? Half the women in the Borders are not entire when they are wed, without ever having known a man.'

'How?' I felt hope rise inside me.

'You ride astride your horse,' Mother said flatly. 'Think what that could do to you.'

'Oh?' I looked at Mother as if I had never seen her before, which in a way I had not. I had known the mother but not the woman. 'Mother: are you saying I should not tell my husband the truth?'

'You tell your husband what he needs to know and what he already knows,' Mother said. 'You tell him nothing that he can use to your disadvantage.'

'Yes, Mother.' My mother had run my father's tower and lands all my life without ever, to my knowledge, betraying his trust. Her wisdom was not to be ignored. Yet I did not wish to live a lie with a man who I trusted and who would trust me.

'You are worried about not being honest with Robert,' Mother said.

'I am,' I said.

'Then let me tell you that your best friend Kate Hunnam has been making sheep's eyes at your good friend Robert for the past few months.'

I smiled. I knew Robert better than Mother did. 'That won't matter to Robert. He is not very interested in women.'

Mother raised her eyebrows. 'He may not be very interested in you, Jeannie. He seems to be very interested in Kate.'

I felt myself stiffen. 'Are you sure, Mother?' I knew she would not tell me if she was not sure.

I cannot write how I felt. I can only write what I did. I turned on my heel and left Cardrona Tower with more anger in me than I had ever felt before. It was not the same feeling as I had with Hugh. That anger had been tempered and controlled, however passionate my love-making had been. This new anger was all-consuming. If Mother was right, then Robert and Kate had been at least contemplating something behind my back for some time. My mistake with Hugh was sudden; theirs was calculated.

I grabbed Kailzie who had served me so well in escaping from Liddesdale, did not bother with saddle, bridle, or stirrups and ordered the gatekeeper to open for me in a snarl that he did not recognise as coming from the laughing girl he knew as Jeannie. I remember that mad dash down the Lethan Valley with the little cottages all getting ready for the night and the river flowing soft and sweet at my side as I whipped that poor horse along. There was an owl calling although I did not hear its mate, and I paid no heed to the surprised but friendly greetings of the people I knew so well. My mind was so filled with the thoughts of betrayal, of my best friend Kate with my chosen man Robert, that I nearly forgot my own treachery as I rode, mouth open and hair flowing behind me.

Whitecleuch Tower is situated on a small knoll, a knowe as we term it, not far from the opening of the valley. It is set above the floodplain of the river with very solid stone walls and a stout barmekin.

The gatekeeper knew me well enough not to challenge my entry even at that time, and I jumped off Kailzie, ordered a surprised and sleepy servant to care for him and was soon bounding up the stairs two at a time to the great hall. It was empty except for two young servants sharing the straw with a few dogs, and one scared kitchen maid with her sweetheart crouched in a corner.

'Where is the young master,' I demanded, more imperiously than I had ever been in my life. I had not realised that my mother's blood was strong within me. I may be a Tweedie, but I was also my mother's daughter. 'Where is Robert Ferguson?'

The servants cowered away from the look in my eyes, or possibly from the horse whip I forgot that I still carried.

'Upstairs, my lady.' The kitchen maid quavered, as her sweetheart put a protective arm around her. Good man, that.

'In his quarters?' I asked.

'Yes, my lady,' the kitchen maid said and added bravely, 'I think it best if you did not enter unannounced...'

'I do not care what you think best,' I told her brutally as I stormed out of the hall and on to the turnpike staircase. Now Whitecleuch is an older tower than Cardrona, with a square central keep much damaged and repaired by war. It was built in the very old days before King Edward Longshanks of England began the series of wars between his nation and ours that has so ravaged the Borderlands. As it predates these savage wars, the walls are less defensive and the windows wider, so allowing more light inside. I ran up the worn stairs with barely a pause and nearly ran into Archie Ferguson himself.

'Jeannie!' He held a flaming torch up high and eyed me with something like alarm, as well he might: a raggle-headed, angry, whip-carrying woman running up the turnpike of his home. 'What are you doing here?'

I took a deep breath to calm my pounding heart. 'I am coming to see Robert,' I said as calmly as I could.

'At this hour? And dressed so?' He seemed astonished.

I realised that I was wearing my indoor clothes. In those days, you see, we did not stand so much on formality in the Borderlands. I wore little more than a shift, a pair of boots, and a shawl. I had not intended to receive visitors and had certainly not expected to be riding down to Whitecleuch in the dimming of the day. 'It was not planned,' I said.

'I don't believe he is at home,' Archie Ferguson said. He was ayeways a bad liar.

'I do believe he is,' I said, 'for I can hear his voice.' That was also a lie of course but I was frantic to see him and put the question to him. 'We are to be wed,' I said foolishly.

As you know, a turnpike staircase, the circular stairs that wind around a central pillar, do not allow much space for manoeuvre, so it was difficult for two people to pass each other. All the same, I pushed forward, squeezing past the grey-bearded old man so that he lost his footing and tumbled down the stairs. I heard him fall, debated with myself whether I should spend the time ensuring he was uninjured, heard him roaring and told myself that a man who made that much noise could not be badly hurt and ran on.

I knew Whitecleuch well of course, as Robert and I had spent our childhood in and out of each other's homes, so I had no difficulty in reaching Robert's chamber. He had shared the topmost turret room with his brother, who was now so sadly departed, and the door was closed and the internal latch down. However, Robert and I had long perfected the trick of inserting a finger under the opening of the latch and hooking it open. I did so now, thrust open the door and pushed it open as hard as I could.

'Robert Ferguson!' I bellowed, waving my whip, 'what is this nonsense I hear about you and Kate making sheep's eyes at each other...' and then I stopped.

My Mother had been entirely correct. Robert and Kate had been making game of me, with more than looks, poetry, and coy imaginings. When I walked in, they were heavily engaged in playing the two-backed beast on Robert's bed. That was why they had not heard the racket I had made in the great hall and the noises old Archie had made as he thundered down the turnpike with such roarings and lamentations.

I had a vision of Kate lying underneath with her head back and her wondrous blonde hair fanned out across the pillow, her eyes closed in ecstasy and her legs and arms splayed out as far as they could splay. Robert lay on top with his parts deep within her and his naked back and legs before me.

It was pure instinct that made me act as I did next. I am well aware that the polite thing to do in this new refined age would be to make my apologies and gracefully withdraw, but we were not in a polite age. We were on the old Border where people acted as they saw fit, where insults were met by instant revenge and one wrong word could start a feud that lasted generations. I saw the man that was destined to be my husband lying with the woman that was my best friend and I did not stop to think. Lifting my whip, I landed the lash across his shoulders with all the power I could muster, and I had been brought up with physical labour since I was old enough to walk. I lambasted that man, landing my whip across his back and shoulders half a dozen times as he lay and yelled. I saw the residue of the mark the Yorling had left across his white behind and I added to it with gusto, all the time yelling my hurt and my anger at such a rank betrayal.

To say I was angry would be an understatement. To say that I felt betrayed after our recent conversation in the stables would be partly accurate. There was no doubt that I had the Tweedie Passion; now I knew that it could come out in more than one way. I had chosen Robert and this Judas kiss was more than I could stomach. I will add that there was also a powerful feeling of satisfaction as I saw him writhe and heard him yell under my lash.

When Robert twisted his head around to look at me with those huge, sorrowful, hurt eyes I could not continue, much as I knew he deserved it. I dropped the whip and stood there, panting for breath.

'So, you don't wish to talk to me in front of your friends.' I heard the catch in my voice. 'Yet you can run to this,' I indicated Kate with a lift of my hand, 'this hussy, this whore, this, this...' I struggled for words that would match my anger. 'This town-bred creature.'

I had known Kate for nearly as long as I had known Robert. Her treason hurt nearly as much. I knew that if I remained in this room much longer, I would do something I would truly regret. Robert's sword hung proudly on the wall and for a moment I was sore tempted to blood the blade, so starting a feud between the Tweedies and Fergusons that would rock the Lethan Valley. Instead, I tried to control my passion.

'Robert,' I said, 'you and I have an agreement. We have an arrangement to marry. Together we would rule the Lethan Valley.' I remembered, albeit belatedly, my mother's words. 'My family is doing all they can to ensure that our marriage works. Now you have a choice. Either you have me, or you have this other woman.' I could not bear to speak Kate's name. 'You cannot have us both.'

Turning away I made what I hoped was a dignified exit.

'Now you know.' Archie Ferguson met me part way down the turnpike with fresh blood seeping down his face.

'Now I know.' With my anger quickly dissipating I felt only like crying. I was empty inside.

'Do you still want him?'

'I still want him,' I said. I had no choice, you see; we were destined to be together. And anyway, how could I blame Robert for doing with Kate what I had done with Hugh? In a way, my recent actions had been directed as much at my own weakness as they had at Robert.

Perhaps that is why I was crying like the Lethan Water itself as I rode up the valley, and perhaps that was why I did not head toward Cardrona Tower but westward, into the high stark hills. Somewhere behind me I heard the voice shouting 'I choose you, I choose you' but I did not know if that was Robert calling from the square keep of Whitecleuch or if it came from inside me. At that second, I did not care. I wanted to be alone.

Chapter Fourteen

FALADALE
OCTOBER 1585

I felt the tears burning my eyes as I pushed Kailzie across the Lethan Water. The western hills were darkening yet seemed more welcoming than any of the peel towers or cottages along the valley. It was only a few days since I had returned home and so much had happened in that time that my mind was in total confusion.

I barely knew where I rode that night. I pushed Kailzie above the outfields and into the heather fringe and allowed her to pick her own route after that. To be honest, I did not know what to do.

Even then, deep within me, I knew that things would turn out for the best. I clung to the truth of my vision, I stuck to that truth. Despite my own weakness with Hugh, despite Robert's betrayal with Kate and my mother's abrupt change of attitude, I knew that I would marry Robert. I now knew that it would not be a perfect marriage; I would not have full trust in him after this evening's revelations, and I certainly did not trust myself.

I rode on into the hills with my faithful brown mare carrying me step by step. There was no rain that night. There was nothing except the wind sighing through the heather and the soft gurgle of distant burns. At one time my mare was walking along the summit ridge of Posso Craig, from where Robert's brother had fallen, making him the heir. My mare halted as something gleamed on top of a shrub of heather. I looked down; father's ring lay there.

I lifted it, folded it in my sleeve and continued. At that moment I thought nothing of the incident. My mind was in confusion.

Hugh.

That name sprang into focus. I had to warn Hugh. Although family was paramount, Hugh and I had been through a lot together in a brief space of time. He had saved my life, and I could not allow him to be killed when my father led the Tweedies on a raid. However, if I warned him, I would be putting my father and all my family, including my fiancé and my new-found brother, in danger. Yet there must be a way.

My thoughts wandered from Robert and of the Yorling over to Kate of the fine blonde hair and lusty nature, and back to Hugh again and I knew that there was a way. I just did not want to follow that crooked and dangerous path. But I knew that I would. I remembered Hugh's smile and the way he cared for me, and the passion he raised in me and I recognised that I would do what was necessary, despite, or because of, Robert.

'This way, girl.' I pushed Kailzie with my knees, guiding her now as we took the hill passes over the Heights. I knew these hills well, up to a point, and that point was a slow-gurgling burn where Tweedie land ended and the lands of the Veitches began. I stopped at that brown burn and looked back over the dark roll of hills that I would own: Tweedie land. Ahead was hostile territory and I was alone, unarmed, and unwanted. I knew only that Hugh was there somewhere, but where, I did not know.

Strangely, the Veitch hills were not all that different from the Tweedie hills. They comprised the same mixture of long grassy slopes, heather that hid leg-snaring holes, dark peaty pools of uncertain depth, and sudden scree slopes where the ground fell away to the unseen ground below.

I did not try to force the pace. My mare had been tried and tested in her journey from Liddesdale. She knew exactly what she was doing. I allowed her to walk at her own pace and knew she would find the safest paths, which would always lead somewhere. In this case that somewhere would be owned by the Veitches. I allowed my mind to drift, seeing again the picture of Robert panting astride Kate's wiry body, seeing him wince under my blows, seeing Kate's sneaking glances at me and Robert's appealing brown eyes.

'Name yourself, stranger!'

The voice floated from the dark.

I stopped. I had not thought that I might be challenged. 'Jeannie,' I said and, knowing that I could not give my real surname, I added 'Ninestane.' It was the first name that came to my mind.

'You are late wandering the Heights,' that voice said. 'And coming from Tweedie lands. What do you seek here?'

I remembered one of my mother's sayings. If in doubt, tell the truth. 'I am looking for Hugh Veitch,' I said.

'Which one?' the voice said. 'We have many men of that name. Is it Bessie's Hugh, or Hugh of the Gate, Lugless Hugh, or Hugh Rob...?'

'I don't know his to-name,' I said, for in my time, with so many people sharing a limited number of surnames, most were known by their to-name. I was Bessie's Jeannie Tweedie, although I never called myself that. 'He is about twenty-two with dark hair and...'

'Well met, Jeannie Ninestane.' Hugh appeared from the dark, smiling. 'What the devil are you doing here? And barebacked, I see; don't they have saddles where you come from?'

'Do you know this woman, Hugh?' that voice in the dark asked.

'We have met,' Hugh said, 'she saved my life in Tarras.'

Two more men emerged from the dark. 'What do you wish done with her, Hugh?'

'I'll take her to the tower,' Hugh said. 'You carry on here.' He held out a hand to me. 'Come, Jeannie, and welcome.'

'I must talk to you,' I said urgently, 'Hugh; you have to get away from here.' We were descending a steep path with my mare following Hugh's piebald, both horses picking their own way. It was full dark ahead of us, broken only by flickering lights from scattered cottages and towers.

'It's just like the Lethan Valley,' I said. It was the first time I had seen Faladale, even though it was so close to my home.

'Very similar,' Hugh said. 'Why are you here?'

'To see you,' I said quietly. Now that I had found him, I was not sure how to go about things. 'I have to talk to you.'

'I am listening,' Hugh said.

We stopped on the hillside beside a small waterfall. The sound brought back a host of memories, of Hugh naked and washing as I stood in the shelter of a tree, of what I saw and how I felt, and how I still felt.

'Hugh!' I took hold of his arm, 'you have to get away from here!'

'Why?' He sounded quite amused.

'It's not safe for you!'

'Tell me more once we get inside,' Hugh said. 'Or don't we have time to do that?'

'I don't know,' I said honestly.

'I will take the chance,' Hugh raised his voice. 'It's Hugh! Open the gate!'

We rode through a high arched gate with a brace of spearmen watching us; both acknowledged Hugh's salute.

'They treat you with respect,' I said.

Hugh laughed. 'They know me and my ugly face.'

The interior of the tower was very similar to Cardrona Tower, with the turnpike staircase leading to the great hall on the first floor. There was the same gaggle of servants and dogs sleeping on the same rush-and-straw flooring and the same scrabble to get out of the way when Hugh and I walked in.

'Give us space,' Hugh ordered, 'and bring wine.'

'Who are you?' I asked as the servants hurried to obey.

'I am Hugh Veitch,' Hugh told me.

'Are you the Lord of this tower?' I looked around at the groined ceiling and the carved fireplace, the mixture of tapestries and armaments on the wall, the long tables that ran the length of the room and the cross-table at the top, where Hugh sat as if by right. I could have been in Cardrona, rather than in the home of the fearsome Veitches.

'I am,' he said.

'You are very young to be the lord.'

Hugh screwed up his face. 'I had no choice in it,' he said. 'My father was killed in a raid by the Tweedies and my mother died in childbirth. I was sent away to be brought up by aunts so Faladale had an heir.' He shrugged. 'Some of the rest you know.'

'Oh,' I said. 'I am sorry.' It was the first time I had considered the feud from the other point of view. I had been brought up with the idea that the Veitches were the wicked family who attacked us; I had never really considered that we should be looked on as the aggressors.

'It is the way of the world.' Hugh seemed to accept it. 'It was not your fault so no need for any apology.'

'It was my surname; my family,' I said.

We were silent as servants produced a flagon of French wine and a plate of cold chicken, with that morning's bread and some cuts of salmon and a bowl of apples.

'Eat, drink and tell me why you crossed the hills to see me at this time of night.' Hugh's eyes were as friendly as ever. 'It is hard to know that you are so close, yet we are divided by a waste of hills and your love for another.'

That was undoubtedly the frankest admission I had ever heard from a man.

'I do not love another,' I said quickly, and once again cursed that I could not curtail my tongue. What power had Hugh that he made me speak the truth to him without forethought? I knew the answer of course, but I could not dare again put it into words.

'Yet you will marry your Robert,' Hugh said, 'despite the strictures of your mother.' His smile was a trifle rueful, I thought. 'I remember, you see.'

'Many men do not listen to the cares of women,' I said.

'And some listen all too well, and are hurt by them,' Hugh said softly as if he spoke to himself.

'My mother now wishes me to marry Robert Ferguson,' I heard the sadness in my voice, 'and that quickly.'

'What has changed her mind?' When Hugh poured me wine, candlelight gleamed through the splendid glass. I had seldom seen anything so beautiful.

'Robert is now heir to Whitecleuch,' I said. 'Our marriage will unite the properties and bring more security to the valley.' I looked up at him, reading the pain in his eyes. 'We will be safer from Veitch attacks.'

'This Veitch does not plan any attacks on the lands of the Tweedies,' Hugh told me, 'Yet he would fain capture the brightest jewel in the Lethan Valley and remove one of the leading men.' His voice hardened as he made that last statement.

'Please don't,' I touched his wrist with my hand, feeling a thrill run through me. 'It is hard enough.'

He nodded, 'it is all of that,' he said and, catching his meaning, I felt myself smile despite my thoughts.

'Is Robert Ferguson worthy of you?' Hugh sipped at his wine. A tiny drop spilt from his glass, to fall slow and soft to the table. I wiped the spot away with my fingers and licked them clean, watching him all the while.

'You have a pretty little tongue,' he said absently.

'I have had it for years,' I said. 'And I will not answer your question about Robert. He is a good man in many ways.'

'I know of him,' Hugh said softly.

'What do you know?' I looked up suddenly.

'I know he is a fine horseman and good at fishing, that he is lazy with his arms and spoiled in his person, but kindly by nature and gentle to children and animals.'

I nodded. 'These things are true,' I agreed.

'I also know that he is not a warrior and has no taste for the lance and sword; he is slow of action and prefers horses to women: except for one woman.' His gaze did not stray from my face.

'I am that woman,' I said softly.

'You are not that woman,' Hugh said. 'That woman is Kate Hunnam of the Kirkton. She is blonde of hair, supple of body, and weak of morals. She will make an uncomfortable wife for any man.'

I felt the pain like a knife, twisting inside my heart. 'I know of their friendship,' I said. 'It is not what I wanted to happen.'

'What we want and what we think we want are often two different things,' Hugh told me. 'In my case, I know what I think I want, and I know what I want. They are one and the same and they are sitting opposite me at this table even as we talk.'

I closed my eyes. I knew then, that I wanted the same as him, yet I knew it was impossible. My future lay with Robert, not with Hugh. It was not the future I wished, yet it was destined and there was nothing I could do about it.

'Hugh.' I held his hand urgently as I strove to change the subject to one that I did have the power to control. 'You must get away from here.'

'And why is that?' Hugh's tone altered from sincerity to amusement.

'The Tweedies are coming,' I said.

'I know that,' Hugh said calmly. 'Kate Hunnam has also been romping with Maisie's Hobbie Veitch. She tells him everything and he passes it on to me. My men are waiting for the Tweedies.'

'Oh.' I had not realised the depths of Kate's treachery. I wished I had landed my lash on her. I still wish that, so many years later.

Hugh continued. 'We have plenty of time together, Jeannie. My lads are positioned all along the hill crests at each pass and each opening to my lands. We will meet them with fire and sword.'

'My father... my brother, and Robert are with them,' I said.

'I have given word not to hurt your father,' Hugh said. 'I did not know you had a brother. My intelligence is usually reliable.'

I explained about the Yorling.

'We still have time,' Hugh said. He did not comment on my half-brother. Such relationships were not uncommon. It was a fact of life.

'Time?' I asked, and when I looked into his eyes, I knew exactly what he meant. 'No, Hugh, I can't...' And then I remembered Robert, and how I had treated him. 'No,' I put steel into my voice. 'I won't.'

Yet when Hugh stretched his hand out to me, I took it and followed him up the turnpike stairs to his chamber. I knew it was wrong, I knew I would hate myself later, I knew that I should not, yet I felt that deep thrill of excitement within me, that mingled tingling of pleasure and apprehension and sheer lust.

Hugh's chamber was not like I had expected. I thought it would be a jumble of male things, over-run with dogs, scattered with weapons, and discarded clothing. Instead, it was clean, austere, and cool, with a sturdy bed in one corner and a carved wooden chair beside a small table on which stood a candlestick and three books. I did not know any other men who read books, except the church minister, and the Reverend Romanes was a very infrequent visitor to the Lethan Valley.

The candle pooled its yellow light from the corner of the room, highlighting the firm line of Hugh's jaw and cheekbones.

'You are one of the few men I know who is clean-shaven,' I said, as he led me in by the hand and closed the door behind him.

'You are one of the few women I know who would ride across the hills at night-time to warn an enemy that he may be attacked.'

'You are the only enemy I would ever warn,' I said, watching as he slipped off his jack. His trousers were next, slipping around his hips, yet even now Hugh did not allow them to fall in a shapeless bundle but lifted them neatly and placed them on the back of his chair.

He stood in his shirt, smiling across to me in that neat room, and I knew that there was nowhere else in the world that I desired to be.

'Take your shirt off.' I heard the catch in my throat as I spoke. His breathing was ragged as he did as I asked and stood naked before me. On the last occasion I had seen him like this, we had been inside the Nine Stane Rig high above Liddesdale. Now we were in Hugh's own chamber in his own tower, yet I felt the same tension as my eyes devoured him. He was all man.

I felt that same surge of passion that chased away reason. I knew that my father could lead the men of the Lethan Valley to attack the Veitches at any time; I knew that Robert could be in danger, yet at that moment I did not care. Only one emotion possessed me, and it centred on the man who stood opposite, watching as I slowly undressed.

I was not afraid and nor was I shy. I wanted him to see me, as I wished to see him. I wanted him to savour my body as I savoured his.

'You are beautiful,' he said when I discarded the last vestige of my clothing and stood before him, proud in my femininity.

After that, we did not talk. We were there, the bed was there, and time was limited. War could take second place to love; nature knows which is more important. There is no need to go into many details about what happened next; you all know what goes where when man meets maid, and Hugh had an urgency that nearly matched my own as we put hands on each other and slid onto the bed.

Our coupling at Nine Stane Rig had been under the gentle rain of autumn; this time we were in the cool shelter of Hugh's chamber with the candle pooling its yellow light over his austere room and our urgent bodies. I pushed him to the bed and mounted him without the need for words, glorying in our healthy, natural desire as he thrust to meet me.

He looked up at me, not smiling. 'I want you,' he said.

'You have me,' I told him, gasping.

There were a few moments of silence except for small sounds of passion and then louder sounds, mainly from me.

We lay together with one of his hands on my bottom and the other around my back as I nestled against his deep chest with its fine crisp hair.

'I do not have you,' Hugh said at last. 'I only have part of you.'

I gave a small giggle that was very unlike me as I glanced down where we were still joined together. 'A very important part,' I said.

'Very important indeed,' Hugh agreed, wriggling that part of him slightly but delightfully. 'But I want more than that.'

'What more do you want?' I asked.

'Your heart,' Hugh said. 'And all the rest.'

I glanced at the door, hoping that Robert did not burst in, as I had with him. 'You know that you cannot have that,' I said.

'I know that,' Hugh said. 'Yet I want it more than ever.'

'It would not be right,' I said, knowing that what we had just done was equally wrong.

'It would be very right,' Hugh said.

I removed his hand from my rump. 'I know it will not happen,' I said. 'I have told you of my vision.'

'That vision could be wrong.' Hugh replaced his hand exactly where it had been. He began to move his fingers, sending little waves of pleasure through me.

'Don't do that,' I said, meaning the exact opposite.

Hugh read the real meaning behind my words. His fingers continued to knead and then began to explore further. I closed my eyes and forgot about everything else.

The smell of smoke awoke me. I felt my nose twitch and coughed, once, twice, and again. I sat up with a jerk, looking around me. The candle had burned to a mess of tallow that had melted over the pewter candlestick and grey dawn had brought patchy mist and rain. The bed was empty save for me and sweet memories.

I sat up. Somebody had pulled a cover over me, lifted my clothes from the floor and folded them neatly on top of his table. That must have been Hugh. I dressed quickly as the smell of smoke increased, now joined by the crackling of fire.

'Is anybody there?' I opened the door and coughed violently. The turnpike stairway was filled with smoke and the sound of burning was obvious. 'Hello?'

There was no reply. 'Hugh?'

Footsteps sounded on the turnpike as a female servant scurried down. I put both hands on her shoulder to stop her. She looked at me, wild-eyed, with her simple one-piece gown filthy and her hair tangled across her face.

'What's happened?' I asked, 'where is everybody?'

She stared at me blankly. I slapped her face, hard. 'Where is Hugh? What has happened?'

She cowered away, obviously too confused or terrified for coherent thought. I let her go and stumbled down the stairs, nearly tripping in the thick smoke. 'Hugh!'

There was another servant in front of me. I took hold of his shoulder. 'Hey, fellow!'

He looked over his shoulder. 'Who are you?'

'Never mind that,' I snapped, 'tell me what has happened? Where is Hugh?'

'We're under attack,' the man said, 'can you not smell the smoke?'

'Where's Hugh?' I shook him, 'where is he?'

When the man shook his head, I threw him away and shouted, 'Hugh!'

The only reply was a fresh billow of smoke and the increasing crackle of fire. I coughed again, waved my hand in front of my face in a futile attempt to see better and realised that unless I got out of the tower I could be smoked to death or burned alive. I moved to an arrow-slit window, took a deep breath of slightly fresher air and dived downstairs, gasping as the heat increased. The entire lower floor was ablaze with the straw and wooden fixtures in the storeroom catching fire.

'This way!' One of the servants had lowered a rope from a first-floor window. 'One at a time.'

I saw the man, a kitchen skivvy, a nothing, somebody that I would pass in the tower without a look or a second glance, yet here he was in the middle of a fire, saving lives at the risk of his own.

'Is there anybody out there?' he asked me.

'I saw a manservant and a maid come down the turnpike,' I said.

'They're out, so we're the last. Get out first.' He pointed to the rope. Rather than argue, I did as I was told and waited on the ground to help the servant down.

'Where is Hugh?' I asked as he landed beside me.

'All the fighting men are riding,' he was about fourteen, with prominent freckles, 'the valley is under attack.'

I nodded. So, Father had arrived and was burning his way along the valley as he had promised. I had failed in my attempt to save Hugh; the Tweedie Passion had taken me over, despite all my good intentions.

Grey dawn streaked the sky, laced with pillars of smoke from fires the breadth and length of the Veitch lands. I sighed; I had not known that Father would be so ruthless in his attempt at eradicating Veitch power.

As I stood outside that tower, I realised with a jolt that I recognised this place. This was where Robert would prove his love for me. This was where my vision took place. The servants approached, three of them, unarmed, smoke-stained and scared; they knew me for a woman of gentle blood and, although they were eminently capable of making decisions for themselves, years of habit had ingrained in them that I should take charge.

'My lady! The Armstrongs are here!'

Armstrongs! Not my father then?

I looked around. Wild Will and a group of his men appeared from behind a copse of trees. I had nearly forgotten them since we left Liddesdale, and now here they were, pursuing their feud with the Veitches. For one moment I wondered how they had got past the watchmen, and then I recalled that Hugh had posted his men to watch over the boundary with the Tweedies. The Armstrongs would have come from the south and west, rather than the east and north. The Armstrong attack could not have come at a worse time. My father, in his quest to quell the Veitches before my wedding to a weak man, had created a situation where Faladale had been exposed to a much more powerful surname.

'You!' Wild Will reined up. He pointed his lance directly at me. 'You and Hugh Veitch set Buccleuch on Liddesdale. I lost five men in that raid!'

I remembered that gallant blade who led the Scott riders. I had not thought of that incident since. Now it had come back to haunt me. I closed my eyes, unable to prevent the inevitable. *Now come to me, Robert, and prove yourself worthy.*

I was in a shallow valley, with the wind whispering through coarse grass. Nearby there was a peel tower, slowly smouldering and sending wispy, acrid smoke to a bruised sky. I was lonely and scared, although there were many men around me. One man approached me; tall, lean, and scarred, he had a face that could chill the fear from a nightmare and eyes sharp and hard enough to bore through a granite cliff.

I backed away, feeling the fear surge through me, knowing that there was nowhere to run. I heard cruel laughter from the men around, rising above the crackle of flames and the lowing of reived cattle.

'Come here.' His voice was like death; cracked, harsh, with an accent from the West.

I did not come. I backed further away until whipcord arms stopped me, holding me tight. I was held and then pushed forward toward the scarred man. I tried to face him, to talk my way out of trouble but the words would not come. My tongue failed me when it was most needed.

'Come here,' the scarred man repeated. He stood with his legs apart, his thumbs hooked into his sword belt and those devil eyes searing into my soul.

'I will not come,' I said.

He stepped towards me, slowly and with each footstep sinking into the springy grass. A gust of wind sent smoke from the fire around him, so he appeared to be emerging from the pits of hell. He let go of his belt and extended his hands toward me. They were long-fingered, with nails like talons, reaching out to grab me. I tried to pull backwards, to ease further away.

I was held again, surrounded by harsh laughter.

My nightmare was about to get worse.

The single shout broke the spell and we all looked to the west, where a lone rider had appeared on the hill crest. Silhouetted against the rising sun, I could not make out details. I only saw a tall, slender man on a horse with a banner in his hand. He stood there for a second with his horse prancing, its fore hooves raised and kicking at the air, and then he plunged down toward me, yelling something, although, in my vision, I could not make out the words.

'Robert!' I said and knew that all would be well.

Here it was; here was the moment when Robert would save me. I saw the rider approach, saw him in silhouette, bold and strong.

'Robert,' I said. I had left him in a fit of anger, yet he had come to my aid. After all the doubts and all the ridicule he had suffered, Robert was proving himself the man I always knew he was.

Other riders came behind him, four, five, six men riding hard, shouting a slogan I could not make out against the sound of the burning tower and the snarls of Wild Will and the Armstrongs.

Wild Will pointed to me. 'Kill her!' he ordered.

One man lifted his lance and moved toward me. He was neither smiling nor full of hatred. My life or death did not matter to him: killing me was merely business, like slaughtering a sheep or robbing a house.

'Robert!' I screamed. I did not run. I knew I would be saved but Robert was taking his damned time about it. I looked to the hills, right into the glare of the rising sun. Robert was tall and bold and strong as he rode straight down the slope, lance couched.

Wild Will rode to meet him, with his men at his back. Somebody drew a dag, a heavy pistol, and fired, with the crack loud amidst the drumming of hooves. None of the advancing riders fell.

And then a cloud slid across the sun and I could see again.

'Robert!' I yelled.

In my vision, I had heard my own voice. I had convinced myself that Robert had come to save me, because I had shouted for him, but it was not Robert. It was Hugh and he rode straight at Wild Will without hesitation. That was not part of my vision, or was it? I had seen that rider race down the hillside so often and had heard my own voice shout 'Robert' so often that I had convinced myself that was his identity. Now I knew it was not he.

The horses of Hugh and Wild Will slammed into each other in a frenzy of flying hooves and tossing manes. Both men discarded their lances, drew swords, and clashed again, blade to blade and face to face as Hugh's followers rode into the other Armstrongs. I saw Hugh pressed backwards as the scar-faced Armstrong used his superior experience and slashed at his thighs. Hugh defended vigorously but it was obvious that Wild Will was the better swordsman.

I ran forward, hoping to help, unsure what to do. Lifting a stone, I aimed it, ready to throw, just as Hugh pulled hard on his reins. His horse reared, flailing with its fore hooves. Wild Will pulled back a fraction, which gave Hugh sufficient space to slice upward with his sword. The point of the blade took Wild Will under the chin and drove on into his brain. He died without a word.

With the loss of their leader, all the fight went out of the Armstrongs. Some of them turned away at once, with others throwing down their weapons in surrender. As more Veitches appeared from the crest of the hill, Armstrongs' withdrawal became a rout and the valley became a scene of flying reivers and pursuing Veitches.

Hugh gave me a huge grin. 'I left you in charge of the house,' he said, 'and look at the mess you made of it.'

'You saved me again,' I said as all the certainties of my images vanished.

'It seems that I also left you to be burned,' Hugh raised his voice. 'Sound the horn; bring the boys back!'

The long ululation sounded across the valley, echoing from the distant hills, eerie, somehow pagan, a call from savage nature. I saw the Veitches halt their pursuit in ones and twos and small groups.

'Sound it again,' Hugh ordered, and the horn blasted out a second time, lifting the small hairs on the back of my neck.

The Veitches returned and gathered around us. I looked at them, these men who were enemies of my blood, and they looked most remarkably like the men with whom I had lived all my life. Young men and old, youths whose chins had never yet felt the scrape of a razor and men with grey beards, long faces, and broad faces, any one of them could have farmed in the Lethan Valley or fitted into the ranks of the Tweedies without comment or concern. As the riders gathered, women emerged from their hiding places to congregate near their men.

'Hugh!' somebody shouted, 'why have you called back the men? We had them on the run!'

'That is why.' Hugh pointed to the crest of the hills on the west, from where rank after rank of men emerged, so their lance points looked like a forest of naked trees. 'It is a common Armstrong trick to pretend a retreat and ambush those who followed when they were scattered and in disarray.'

I watched the Armstrongs as they re-entered the valley. I had thought that this was only a raid by Wild Will and his outlaws. Now I knew that it was a full-scale attack; the Armstrongs had brought their full might to end their feud with the Veitches.

'A Tweedie!' The call came from behind us and we turned around.

'A Tweedie! A Tweedie!' My father had, at last, arrived, bringing all the manpower of the Lethan Valley with him.

'We are surrounded,' the voice was panicky. 'The Tweedies have joined the Armstrongs against us! Run for your lives!'

Hugh looked at me, and for the first time since I had known him, he looked worried. 'I fear we are caught between two fires,' he said. 'Your people have arrived at a most inopportune moment.'

I nodded as the fear rose within me. With the Armstrongs in front, smarting at the death of Wild Will, and my own surname in the rear, determined to finish their feud, there seemed little hope for the Veitches. I took a deep breath. 'Ride with me,' I said, grabbed Wild Will's loose horse and kicked toward the advancing Tweedies.

No doubt convinced that I had gone mad, Hugh joined me and we rode toward Father's men.

I halted a hundred paces in front of them and raised my hand. 'Father! I would have a word before any killing starts!'

Father had indeed been busy. Judging by the numbers, he had raised every man in the Lethan Valley, from cubs barely in their teens to grey and even white-bearded men who must first have held a lance when Queen Mary was a toddling infant. At one side of him, resplendent in his yellow jack, rode the Yorling. At the other was Robert, frowning as he glowered at me.

'I see you have thrown in your lot with the enemy,' Robert said. 'My fault was minor when I bedded Kate. Yours is rank betrayal.'

'This is not because of your poor choice.' I was very aware of the men lining up in front of me, ready to plunge lance and sword into Hugh and ravage his already burning valley. I turned a cold shoulder to Robert. 'We can talk later,' I said, 'there are more important matters than your desires.'

'The killing has already begun.' Father was in full war attire with padded leather jack straining against his full belly and a lance that had seen service at Langside. 'Your new friends have brought fire and blood to the Lethan.'

'They have not,' I said as the full picture opened before me. 'The Veitches have not attacked the Lethan. The Armstrongs have attacked us both, I think.'

Father frowned. He knew I would never lie to him. I was not good at that noble art. 'Is that the Armstrongs over there?' He gestured with his lance past the assembled Veitches and toward the too-rapidly advancing horde of Armstrongs.

'It is,' I said. 'They are burning the Lethan because I escaped from Wild Will and are burning Faladale in pursuit of their feud with the Veitches.'

Father rode forward, gesturing to the Yorling to remain in place. Robert made no move to join him.

'You are Hugh Veitch of Roberton,' he said.

Of *Roberton*? I stared at Hugh. I had not known that his house was named Roberton. So, my vision had been correct all the time. I had been rescued by a man with the name of Robert, except it was not the Robert I had expected. I would have laughed if we had not all been in imminent danger of being gutted by an Armstrong lance.

'I am Hugh Veitch, once of Roberton, now of Faladale,' Hugh replied steadily. 'And you are Tweedie of Lethan. We are blood enemies from some long past dispute.'

Father nodded, looked to me and shook his head. 'What are you doing here, girl?'

'I am no longer a girl,' I replied, 'I am full woman, and Hugh is my chosen man.' It was perhaps not the best time and place to announce my intention, but beggars can't be choosers and anyway, there was a very good chance that we would all be dead in a very short space of time. Best to get these things out in the open when one is still alive, I thought, rather than dying with the truth untold.

The Armstrongs were closer now, around seven hundred lances, all experienced in the bloody feuds of Liddesdale, hard men who had kept the Border aflame for generations, reivers used to warfare and plunder. Yet we ignored them as we discussed our own disputes and alliances.

'I see.' Father looked lost; I doubted if he understood half what was going on. He looked to the advancing Armstrongs, and at the gathered Veitches, many of whom glanced nervously over their shoulders or at the hills that might provide refuge if they fled. 'I think, Hugh of Roberton, that we should set aside our differences and settle with the Armstrongs first.'

'That would be best,' Hugh agreed. 'I do not know why we are at feud anyway.'

Father grinned. 'I have long forgotten the reason,' he said. 'I will take the left flank of the Armstrongs.'

'And I the right.' Hugh's smile was back. 'The centre can care for itself!' He looked at me. 'You keep out of the way, Bessie's Jeannie Tweedie. We have much to discuss when this battle is won.'

'I never use that name,' I told him, but he had already turned his horse and was leading his men toward the Armstrongs, shouting his war cry: 'A Veitch! A Veitch!'

I doubt you have ever seen a battle fought by Border horse, or prickers as we termed them. It is not like any other encounter that you can imagine. I stood with the Veitch women, watching as our menfolk rode to defend us, and like them, I feared for the safety of my men.

Hugh led his Veitches splendidly. I watched his every move as the combined army of Tweedies and Veitches advanced in a single mass, only to split in two when they were three hundred paces from the Armstrongs. Now, normally Border horsemen use subterfuge and cunning when they fight. They used feigned retreats and sudden ambushes, false noises in the dark and ruses to upset and confuse their enemy. This battle had none of that. The Armstrongs came in force, angry at the death of Wild Will and my people of both surnames were fighting to defend their land. And us, their women.

As Hugh led his Veitches in a glorious charge against the Armstrong left flank, Father was in front of the Tweedies. I watched, unable to tear my gaze from the scene as all my men crashed into the Armstrong ranks. I heard Father's bellow even above the roar and clamour of battle. I saw the Yorling, my half-brother, leading his band of callants in a mad dash that turned the very tip of the Armstrong army and pushed it back before he wheeled his horse round to hit them in their exposed flank. I saw Robert, my foolish, clumsy, spoiled Robert, fight manfully with the rest. Oh, he was slow and weak compared to some but when it mattered, he had turned up and he did his best for the surname. He did not disgrace himself on that day of bold deeds and bloody carnage. I was proud of my Robert, as I always knew I would be. Except he was no longer my Robert; he was Kate's Robert and he would be a good husband to her, and she a poor wife to him.

Most of all I watched Hugh. By that time, I knew that he had been the man in my vision: Hugh Veitch of Roberton. The name had a ring to it. It still has a ring to it, don't you think? It is a fine name and he led the Veitches with pride and valour. Of course I was scared for him, but on the Border, women knew that men would go to reive and to war. That was the way of the world. It always had been and we could not see it ever changing. We were proud of the hardihood of our men and of the deeds of our surnames. I was no different to all the rest, and why should I be?

My Hugh fought in the van, carving his way through the ranks of the Armstrongs, out the other side and then guiding his men into that flank attack that scattered the enemy. I saw the Armstrong army break up as men on the fringes decided that flight was preferable to death or capture. Others joined them in sudden dismay. They had come looking for plunder and destruction, not for hard fighting against a determined foe.

All at once the Armstrong array crumbled and collapsed. They turned and fled and this time neither Hugh nor my father called halt to the dogs of war. The combined Veitch-Tweedie force pursued them into the tangled hills that surrounded our valleys, and I dare say that many of the Armstrongs did not return to their sinister Liddesdale again.

I did not watch the pursuit. I did not have to. I knew that all of my men were safe and that is all that mattered to me. As I waited for their return, I wondered what Mother would have to say about everything. And I thought of Hugh of Roberton.

Chapter Fifteen

AT HOME
MAY 1586

We married in the ancient chapel at Laverlaw at dawn on Beltane Sunday. Hugh looked decidedly uncomfortable in doublet and hose, with no sword at his side and in a place with bad memories of past betrayal. I had chosen Laverlaw for that reason: the best way to remove a bad memory is to replace it with a better one. I ensured that there would be no bad memories this time, as our marriage cemented the two surnames of Tweedie and Veitch into a single family.

I tried to get Hugh to drop his name of Veitch in favour of Tweedie, but he refused.

'I have always been Hugh Veitch and Hugh Veitch I will remain,' he said, adding a slow kiss to sweeten his words. I welcomed that kiss and continued it to its natural conclusion with a mad encounter that left us both gasping and in disarray and the bedclothes a rumpled mess.

Afterwards, we toasted ourselves in honey mead and laughter as we adjusted each other's clothing and righted the bed.

'What will the maids say?' Hugh wondered.

'They would be jealous of me,' I said truthfully and failed to stifle my girlish giggle. 'More to the point, what would my mother say?'

'She would say that you are using the Tweedie Passion for its rightful ends,' Mother's voice came from the doorway. I looked up in a mixture of dismay and embarrassment, wondering how much she had heard and, more to the point, how much she had seen.

'Mother!' I smoothed my skirt across my lap and attempted to look innocent.

'It's a bit late for that, Jeannie,' Mother said, although the twinkle in her eye proved she was not displeased. 'I expect you two to produce a dozen grandchildren for me. I only had the one daughter; I want sons and daughters enough to populate both our valleys and some left over.'

'Mother! Please!' I was genuinely scandalised that my mother should say such things.

Hugh, however, was not abashed. 'We will do our best to oblige,' he said, laying his hands on me in a manner that even husbands-to-be should not do in front of their mother-in-law. Or, indeed, in front of anybody else.

I slapped him down, pushing his hands away, trying not to laugh in front of Mother.

'Now that your father has to rebuild Cardrona Tower to my standards after the Armstrongs destroyed it, I need willing hands to help so the quicker you two get producing the better.' She turned away and spoke over her shoulder. 'It is good to have you in the family, Hugh. I never had much time for Robert Ferguson; he was and is no match for my Jeannie.'

'You were going to have me marry him, Mother,' I reminded.

'That was family business, Jeannie,' she said. 'I was acting as matriarch of the Tweedies, not as your Mother. Please God, you never have to make the same distinction.'

There were green boughs around Laverlaw Chapel for the wedding, with early laverocks singing high above and all the leading families of both surnames present to witness this historic union that ended a blood feud that had lasted centuries. I was in a bit of a dream that day, unsure if it was truth or fantasy as I prepared for my wedding.

When Robert Ferguson arrived, I kissed him for the first and last time, and I apologised for ill-treating him so badly that day I discovered him with Kate Hunnam of the Kirkton.

'It does not matter,' Robert told me. 'We are to be married later this year.'

'I am glad of it,' I told him, and I meant it. Now that our respective matrimonial disputes were resolved I had no quarrel with Robert. 'I wish both of you all the happiness in the world,' I said.

'As I do to you,' he responded at once, with the generosity that was typical of him, although he was more prone to show it to horses rather than to people.

After the kiss, I shook his hand and gave Kate a slight nod. That was all I would spare for the woman who had been a friend and who had betrayed me. What we had once was now spoiled and would never return. We both accepted that without another word being uttered. I wished I had taken the opportunity to lay the whip across her flesh when I had the chance: that was my only regret. I think that I have wasted sufficient words on Kate Hunnam and I will move on to happier things than those concerning that woman.

Naturally, my father posted half a dozen riders around the chapel to ensure that nobody took advantage of the peaceful nature of the wedding. Perhaps they did their job well or maybe word had got out that the combined Tweedie-Veitch surname would brook no interference; either way we were left alone. After defeating the Armstrongs there were few surnames who would care to beard us in our own land. Indeed, we were now one of the more respected names on the Border.

We brought in the minister from Peebles to perform the ceremony, and while he was there we sang doleful psalms to celebrate our union. The Reverent Romanes was a broad-shouldered man with an eye for the ladies, yet his attention did not stray for an instant when he was surrounded by the hard-riding Tweedies and Veitches.

'Are you sure you wish to go ahead with this marriage?' my father asked me.

I nodded. 'I have never been more sure in my life,' I said.

He gave a small smile that hid huge amusement. 'I remember you being equally sure you wished to marry Robert Ferguson.'

'I was younger then,' I told him solemnly.

'You were,' Father said. 'That was all of eight months ago. Will you become a Veitch? There was some worry in his voice.

'I will not,' I said. 'I was born Jean Tweedie and I will die Jean Tweedie.' That is a thing we do in Scotland: in other places, when a woman marries, she loses her surname; in Scotland, she keeps her own name and fortune. I am still Jean Tweedie, although now my husband is Hugh Veitch.

I wore a fine light-blue gown that had belonged to my mother, with a circlet of flowers to lighten my black hair and shoes so tight they damn nearly crippled me. I kicked them off at the first opportunity, I can tell you. Fashion is all very well but not when it interferes with comfort. I am mistress of a Border surname, not some pampered and powdered lady from an Edinburgh townhouse. I have not seen these shoes since so I suppose that some lucky young girl saw them on the floor and appropriated them for her own wedding at some distant time in the future. Either that or Robert took them to re-use the leather for his horses. Certainly, they would not fit Kate, as her feet are as large as her desires for men. Poor Robert: I hope his love for horses compensates for his wife's love of playing the two-backed beast around the Borders. I do not interfere: it is none of my business.

Father was watching with an indulgent smile on his face. I stepped over to him and whispered in his ear. 'I have been holding this for you.' I slipped his ring inside his fist. 'You must have lost it when you pushed Robert's brother over Posso Craig.'

Father took the ring without demur. 'It was the best way to get your mother to accept him as your husband,' he said.

'Thank you, Father.' I kissed him and returned to Hugh. As I have said before, murder was acceptable in the old Border, as long as it was for a good reason.

'I hope you are both very happy together.' The Reverend Romanes glanced around at the growing clamour as Father introduced mead and French claret to the crowd.

'We will be,' Hugh said. He held out his hand. 'Thank you for your services, Minister.'

The Reverend Romanes took the hand somewhat gingerly. 'You are part of my flock,' he said.

'If you ever need a favour, Minister,' Hugh said, 'you let me know. A rival church burned, a sinner killed, anything like that, I am your man.'

I swear I saw a twinkle in the good Reverend's eye. There was a man there, beneath the solemnity. I wondered viciously if Kate had noticed. If so, she would have the ministerial robes off him quicker than he could say grace. 'I don't believe I will require either of these services,' the Reverend said.

After the minister returned to care for the spiritual wellbeing of his more restrained parishioners, no doubt thankful to have survived intact among us wild men and women of the valleys, we began the real festivities. The ale, mead, and wine flowed free as a pair of Border pipers arrived to add their music. I saw my half-brother dancing with Kate and wished him well. I knew that Robert would be in the stables with his horses and did not interfere.

They say that the partying lasted two weeks and that may well be true. I cannot tell, for after only twelve hours of dancing and general laughter, Hugh took me by the hand and led me upstairs to our chamber. I felt my mother's eyes following me and wriggled my hips to her, waved a hand behind my back and climbed the turnpike to prove yet again that I had my full measure of the Tweedie Passion.

I knew I would have many hundreds of occasions to test that in the years ahead, and with the man I would choose above all others.

But at night, when the moon is full and a wind stirs the branches in the trees, I sometimes start awake and think of that night on the Nine Stane Rig, when Hugh first awakened the Tweedie Passion within me. And then I roll over, reach for him in the dark and prove that it has not gone away. It never shall; not between me and my man, my Hugh Veitch of Roberton.

Historical Note

There is no Lethan Valley in the Scottish Borders, but there is a Manor Valley, on which I based the location. The topography is much as I described, and at one time there were ten peel towers dotted along the valley floor. The remains of three survive, two ruined and one nearly intact.

There was a feud between the Tweedies and the Veitches, who held neighbouring lands near the Tweed. As with all Border feuds, there was bloodshed and murder involved and nobody was quite sure how it started. My own account is entirely fictional. The story of the Spirit of the Tweed is part of local folklore, although I added a slight twist.

The Armstrongs of Liddesdale were indeed one of the most feared riding—or reiving—families of the Border. They were not a surname to cross: names such as Ill Will Armstrong, Kinmont Willie, and Johnnie Armstrong are still remembered in song and ballad.

The Wolf Craigs exists as I have described, although I shifted the location from the Pentland Hills, where I courted my own love.

The Nine Stane Rig and the associated folklore also exists, exactly where I have placed it. It is a fascinating, uncanny place which can be visited. Not all can sense the atmosphere, but for those with the feelings, it is not a place to miss. Take a copy of Scott's *Border Ballads* when you visit and listen for the ghosts.

The lifestyle along the Border was much as I have described. It was a lawless frontier where raid and feud ruled, and it seems that cynical kings in both Edinburgh and London preferred that: they used the border counties as a buffer between their respective countries, and the wild men and women of the hills and valleys were always useful in time of war. Only when King James VI of Scotland took over the English throne was there a hope of peace in the old Border, and when that happened in 1603, a sort of peace descended. Yet there can still be an uneasy atmosphere in the southernmost counties of Scotland and it is best not to push these men and women too hard, lest the old, not-quite-dormant spirit comes out again and the call 'A Tweedie!' or 'An Armstrong!' echoes from the long green hills.

Helen Susan Swift
July 2016

Dear reader,

We hope you enjoyed reading *The Tweedie Passion*. Please take a moment to leave a review, even if it's a short one. Your opinion is important to us.

Discover more books by Helen Susan Swift at
https://www.nextchapter.pub/authors/helen-susan-swift

Want to know when one of our books is free or discounted for Kindle? Join the newsletter at http://eepurl.com/bqqB3H

Best regards,

Helen Susan Swift and the Next Chapter Team

You might also like:

A Turn of Cards (Lowland Romance Book 3) by Helen Susan Swift

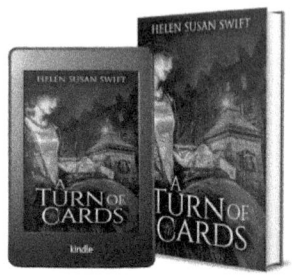

To read first chapter for free, head to:
https://www.nextchapter.pub/books/a-turn-of-cards

Also by the Author

- The Handfasters (Lowland Romance Book 1)
- The Tweedie Passion (Lowland Romance Book 2)
- A Turn of Cards (Lowland Romance Book 3)
- The Name of Love (Lowland Romance Book 4)
- Dark Mountain
- Dark Voyage
- The Malvern Mystery
- Sarah's Story
- Women of Scotland

Lightning Source UK Ltd.
Milton Keynes UK
UKHW020004180920
370100UK00011B/418